F of China

Jagmohan Chopra

Illustrated by
Susan Harmer

MACMILLAN

First published 1989 by Sterling Publishers Pvt, India.
This edition published 1990, under licence from Sterling Publishers.

Published by MACMILLAN EDUCATION LTD
London and Basingstoke
Associated companies and representatives in Accra, Auckland, Delhi, Dublin, Gaborone, Hamburg, Harare, Hong Kong, Kuala Lumpur, Lagos, Manzini, Melbourne, Mexico City, Nairobi, New York, Singapore, Tokyo.

Printed in Singapore

British Library Cataloguing in Publication Data
Folk Tales of China.
1. Chinese tales
I. Title II. Chopra, Jagmohan
398.21089951

ISBN 0 – 333 – 54522 – 2

Contents

	Introduction	v
1	The giants	1
2	The story of a wise woman	8
3	Why rabbits have pink eyes and long ears	19
4	The old woman	24
5	The mean farmer	28
6	The pearl of honesty	30
7	The twin-headed phoenix	36
8	Bayberry	39
9	The water buffalo	44
10	The bragging tortoise	47
11	The frog	51
12	In search of happiness	56
13	The spirit	60
14	The unsatisfied mason	63
15	The golden vase	66
16	The black spot	70
17	The stealing of Rose-Red	72
18	The little camel	77
19	The shade of the mulberry tree	80
20	The wise man	82
21	A bird with nine heads	85
22	The pole with magic powers	89
23	The teaching of a lesson	92
24	The long-white-haired girl	96

Introduction

Folk tales are a crucial component of folklore, depicting the traditions, customs and beliefs of a country. They reflect the richness, character and freshness of their fertile imagination and cultural ethos. Folk tales also provide a greater insight into the distinctive character, culture, hopes and fears of a people than formal literature.

After the success of an earlier venture, I was inspired by my children and friends to compile this collection of folk tales. As a student of history, I have always been fascinated by the ancient, rich and colourful civilisation of China. This is why I have attempted this book on the folk tales of China.

The tales belong to the olden days of China when heroes, saints and rulers assumed magical powers. Some of the stories deal with the perennial battle between good and evil. These stories offer a deep insight into Chinese life and culture.

I have found that the most important aspect of the folklore of a region is the folk tale — a story which consists of one or more themes and motifs. Folk tales easily pass from one language into other languages, and travel all over the world; hence they are sometimes called 'migratory tales'. Formal literature borrows themes from folk tales and most of the world's greatest writers have incorporated themes from folk tales into their work.

Jagmohan Chopra

1

The giants

Once upon a time there lived a merchant in the south of China. He would sail to distant lands to sell his goods and would on his return bring back precious stones. But on one of his journeys, his ship drifted to unknown lands, because of a great storm. The land was covered with green vegetation and high mountains. When he thought he saw signs of human habitation he went to the shore with some food. On reaching it he saw a line of open caves. He peeped into one of them and found to his horror that they were caves belonging to ogres who had teeth like spears, fiery eyes and sharp claws.

The merchant was terrified and tried to escape but the ogres caught sight of him. They captured him and dragged him to their caves. When the two ogres talked they made sounds like animals. They tore off his clothes and wanted to devour him but the merchant hurriedly gave them the food which he had brought from the ship. The ogres liked the food so much that they wanted more. Then he showed them his empty satchel and told them that he had no more with him but he could bring much more if they would let him go to the ship. The ogres could not understand what he was saying, so they were still very angry. The poor man then tried to make them understand by gestures by which they eventually seemed to comprehend him a little.

They followed him to his ship and he brought his cooking utensils back to the cave, gathered firewood, lit

a fire and cooked the remains of a stag. When it was done, he gave it to them to eat. The two creatures devoured it with great pleasure. They were very pleased with him. After eating they left the cave, but closed the opening with a huge boulder.

This was the first time that the ogres had eaten a cooked meal because their normal diet was raw meat. After some time the ogres came with a huge cauldron and another stag, which they had freshly killed. The merchant skinned it, washed the meat and cooked it well. A large number of ogres gathered there to have a meal which was a novelty for them and after enjoying a hearty meal returned to their own houses. But from that day, the merchant cooked their meals.

Thus several weeks passed and gradually the ogres became very fond of the merchant. They allowed him to roam around. He also picked up their language and was soon able to converse with them in their own tongue. This made the ogres very happy, so out of gratitude, they found an ogre girl for him. The merchant was too scared to go near her but the ogre girl enticed him with her affection and soft manners. Eventually he took her as his wife, and both became very fond of each other.

One day the ogres rose very early and wore necklaces of gleaming pearls round their necks. They also asked the merchant to cook a large quantity of meat. He asked his wife the reason for the festivity and his wife told him that the day was a great feast day for which the ogres had invited their great king to eat with them. When the ogress told the other ogres that the merchant had no pearl necklace to wear, they gave her five pearls apiece and she herself added ten, so that he had over fifty pearls. He threaded them and hung the chain round his neck. Each of these pearls was worth a fortune.

The merchant then started cooking the meat for the feast. After finishing the cooking he left the caves with the ogres to welcome the great king. A large cave was prepared for such occasions, where many ogres could sit. One seat was on a raised platform built for the great king.

Everybody was sitting in their places when suddenly a great storm arose, and a monster, who resembled the ogres in shape strode in. The ogres stood up in great excitement to welcome him. The great king came into the cave, sat down on his seat and looked around with large keen eyes. Then all the ogres took their seats, crossing their arms on their chests to express their respect.

While he was watching the crowd his eyes fell on the merchant and he asked in a thunderous voice: 'Who is he?' His wife answered for him and they all praised his cooking skill. The ogres laid table for the great king, and he ate his fill. With his mouth still full he praised the food and commanded that this dish was always to be served to him. Then he glanced at the merchant and asked him why his necklace was smaller than the necklaces of the other ogres. He took ten pearls from his own necklace which were larger than the others, and gave them to the merchant who crossed his arms and thanked the king in ogre language. With this, the party ended and the great king left, riding away through the air in the storm.

With the passage of time the ogre wife of the merchant bore him triplets, two boys and a girl. They were all like their father. This made him very happy and more attached to his wife and children.

One day, as he was alone in his cave, an ogre female from some other cave came in and tried to seduce him. He resisted her but this made the ogress very angry. Before she could harm him, his wife came in and the two females began to fight fiercely. Eventually, the merchant's wife bit one of the other woman's ears off. Screaming loudly, the ogress left. From then onwards the merchant's wife always guarded her husband and never left him for a moment.

More years passed and the children were learning to speak. The merchant also taught them the human language. They grew up and became so strong that they ran up and down the mountains as though on level ground.

One day, the wife had gone out with the girl and one of the boys, and was not planning to come back before evening. A strong longing for his own country grew in the merchant's heart. He took his son and went to his ship which was still riding at anchor. He boarded it with his son and after a day and night returned to his city.

When he got back he found that in the meantime his first wife had married another man. He sold two of his pearls for such a quantity of gold that he was able to keep an elegant house. He gave his son the name of Panther. At fourteen Panther was so strong that he could lift a thirty hundred weight. But he was rough and fond of quarrels. The general of the army in that country was so impressed by his bravery, that he appointed him colonel in the army. At the tender age of eighteen he was made under-general when he suppressed a rebellion with great strength and bravery.

At about the same time, another merchant was driven by a storm to the island of the ogres. When he stepped on the land he saw a young man who asked him whether he had seen his father. As luck would have it, this merchant belonged to the same place where the young man's father was living. This merchant asked him who his father was. After hearing the name, he told the young man that he knew his father. The boy said to the merchant, 'How nice to hear that you know my father and belong to the same place. Please give my regards to my father and my brother. I really miss them'. On hearing this, the merchant said, 'Young man, as I am on my way to my homeland, why don't you come along with me too and meet your father and brother'.

The young man told the merchant that his mother was different in speech and appearance, so she could not go, and he did not want to leave his mother and sister. With tearful eyes he saw the merchant off on his ship.

When the merchant reached his homeland, he went to the palace of Panther, the under-general and told him of his experience. When Panther heard him speak of his brother he wept bitterly. He took leave and, accompanied by two soldiers, sailed out to sea. Suddenly, there was a storm and Panther fell into the sea. Just before he drowned, two powerful hands seized him. The creature who saved him was an ogre. Panther thanked him in ogre language. Amazed, the ogre asked him who he was and he told him his whole story.

The ogre was delighted to meet him, then he sent him to the ogreland where his mother, sister and brother were living.

When he got there, Panther saw a young man standing on the beach whom he immediately recognised as his brother. Both were very happy to see each other. Now Panther wanted to see his mother and sister. Both the mother and daughter also arrived and on seeing Panther, both wept with emotion. Panther asked them to accompany him back to his father's homeland.

But his mother said, 'Son, I am afraid to go, because I am different from human beings. They will laugh at me because of my appearance.' Panther told his mother not to worry because he was a very high official, and people would not dare offend her.

They began making preparations to sail for their father's land and after a journey of three days, reached land. But all the people ran away on seeing Panther's mother. Panther gave some clothes to three of them to cover themselves. On reaching his palace, the merchant met his wife and children. He was happy to have them with him, but the people were frightened of his wife.

Panther told his mother to wear silks like other women and try to learn their language. With good living conditions, and with good food, both the girl and the boy became as good looking as Panther. The boy was named Leopard and the girl Ogrechild. Both were extremely strong.

Panther did not want his brother to remain uneducated and therefore arranged for him to study. Leopard was exceedingly gifted. Within no time he became a scholar.

But shooting and riding were what he liked best. That is why he made a great military career and eventually married the daughter of a highly respected official.

Because of her mother, Ogrechild had a little difficulty in finding a good husband. But when people saw that she was a very brave and talented girl, one of the officers of the army consented to marry her. She was very good at shooting with a bow and arrow and her aim was infallible. Because of her expertise she would accompany her husband in battle, and it was because of her prowess that her husband rose to the rank of general.

Leopard was so brave and strong that at the young age of thirty he became field marshal and his mother would accompany him on his campaigns. It was because of her that many dangerous enemies were defeated. For her courage, the emperor awarded her the title of 'Greatest of Women'.

For generations to come, the family was known for its strength and bravery. The secret of this was the strength of the ogres combined with the wisdom of the human brain.

2

The story of a wise woman

In a distant village of China, there lived a poor couple who were blessed with a girl. Though poor, they were enriched with a most beautiful and intelligent child. There was magic in the hands of the girl. She could do such fine embroidery that it was difficult to find its equal in the country.

In her mid-teens she fell in love with a man who was also poor but very honest and simple. He was loved by everybody because of his good conduct. Having known each other since childhood, they understood each other well. The parents agreed to the match and the two were betrothed to get married in the spring.

But things do not always turn out as planned. A village is a small place and anything unusual gets talked about. Because of her extraordinary beauty and intelligence this girl became very famous. Her fame travelled far and wide and within no time reached the ears of the king of the country. Apart from hearing of her uncommon looks, the king also came to see the girl's wonderful embroidery.

The king sent his men to the father of the girl to ask for her hand in marriage. The father of the girl told the king's men that his daughter was already betrothed to a man of her choice, so if they wanted to talk about her, they should do so with her only.

So the king's men approached the girl. In vain did the messengers plead the king's suit. The girl politely refused their offer and asked them to go back saying, 'I am most honoured by the king, but I cannot marry him. I am the daughter of a poor man and am betrothed to a poor man too'. The king's men were not happy on hearing the soft-spoken refusal, but they had to go back and tell the king. On hearing what had transpired, the king became very angry and swore to have the girl some day.

When the spring came, she got married to the man of her choice. Both of them worked hard to earn their living. After some time they saved some money and with it she told her husband to buy some thread. The husband bought the thread and his wife busied herself day and night weaving it into four pieces of ribbon. Her fine handiwork was sold quickly, and with this money more thread was bought. This time she made some tapestry. 'This tapestry is going to bring us twenty silver pieces, don't sell it for less than that,' said the girl to her husband. 'Take it to any of the forty streets in town and bring it back if you cannot sell it. But remember that you must not take it to the forty-first street.'

Anyone who saw the tapestry marvelled over it, but as the times were not good, people could not spend twenty silver pieces on some tapestry. The poor husband went round and round the streets, till it became dark, but could not find any buyer. As he was planning to return home he thought that his wife would feel sad if he returned without selling the tapestry. Unconsciously, he entered the forty-first street. The street was lined with tall buildings. It was very quiet there and he did not find a single person walking in the street. All of a sudden he realised that he was near the palace, and was forbidden by his wife to go near the palace. As he was about to retrace his steps, he saw a crowd emerging from the palace gate. It was the king with his courtiers. The king noticed the solitary figure standing in the centre of the street and in his booming voice asked the man who he was. He asked him what he was doing near the palace. Didn't he know that no one was allowed to enter that street?

The poor man was frightened and told the king that he did not know anything about the street but was now going back. The king saw something in his hands and asked him what it was. The man replied that it was some tapestry. The king insisted on seeing it. Immediately, the king recognised the exquisite tapestry made by the beautiful and intelligent girl, whom he had wanted to marry. He asked the husband 'Who made this?' As he was a simple man, the husband could not reply cleverly. He said that he had made it. But when the king asked again he said that his sister had made it. Now the king was getting impatient and told the man if he did not want to suffer, he should spell out the truth. So the husband told the king that his wife had made it.

The king was full of envy. 'So this is the husband she has chosen instead of me. I will never forget this insult', he thought to himself. Aloud he told the husband that he was going hunting and, on his way, would like to halt at his house for some refreshment.

The poor man was very sad and reproached himself for not heeding the advice of his wife. On reaching home he gave the money to his wife, but looked miserable. The wife knew at once that there was something amiss.

She asked her husband, why he was looking so worried. He could not hide anything from her, so told her everything. The poor wife became very sad in the anticipation of something terrible happening. On seeing his wife sad his eyes filled with tears. The pretty wife could not see her husband like that so she consoled him saying, 'Look, dear husband, when the king comes tomorrow, I will hide somewhere. You tell him that I have gone out. Don't worry, let us hope everything turns out well'.

Next day, the king arrived in their house and asked for tea, hoping that the wife of the man would serve it. But to his utter dismay, the man went inside to make the tea. The king asked him to sit with him and let his wife serve the tea. Then the poor man told the king that his wife was not in the house as she had gone somewhere and was not likely to come back for several days. The king became very angry, but did not show his anger. Instead, he asked him to share some wine with him. The simple man could not refuse such an offer from royalty, but before he finished the cup of wine, he fell into a stupor, as the wicked king had drugged the wine with a potion which was so strong that it could put a person to sleep for three to four days.

Then the king ordered a search of the house, and the girl was found hiding. On seeing her, the king was charmed. He found her even more beautiful than he had heard. Forgetting his status and position, he begged the girl to marry him. He promised to provide everything available on this vast earth. But the girl refused, telling the king that she loved her husband and could never love the king, or anyone else.

The king flew into mad rage and ordered his men to carry the girl forcibly to his palace. The girl was clever and knew that if the king took her forcibly, her husband would never know her whereabouts so she had to do something. With this in mind she told the king that she was ready to go with him on the condition that she should be allowed to do a specific ritual of worship to the gods with bread and water. The king was overjoyed to hear that she was willing to go with him on a condition which was so simple and ordinary.

But this worship was not as simple and ordinary as it seemed. In the guise of worship, the girl left indications for the husband so that he could find out where she was.

Doing everything possible, she left with the king for his palace.

After three days, when the husband woke up, he found himself alone. He knew at once that he had been tricked by the wicked king and that his wife had fallen prey to him. Then he saw the bread and the bowl of water with which she had worshipped the gods. But the husband knew that she had put them there for him as clues to help him to find out that she had been taken to the palace by the king. He ate the bread and drank the water and went towards the palace as far as the gates.

The palace was within very high walls and the entrance was guarded by the soldiers. He wandered around the palace for one whole day and night. An old woman saw him and asked him what he was doing there. The woman seemed to be a kind one, so he told her what had happened. On hearing him, the old woman gave him a coin and told him to buy thread, needles, combs, mirrors and other such items. She suggested, 'You could go to the palace gates and peddle your wares. In that way, who knows, you might see your wife'.

In the meantime, the king asked the wife to marry him without delay. The girl told the king that though she had come to the palace, she could not marry him for one month because she had some terrible disease. She also told him to allow her to roam around within the palace to avoid boredom. She told him not to get impatient because she had already come to the palace. The king had to agree with her.

After a few days, the king went hunting and the girl strolled near the palace gates. She heard the voice of a pedlar selling his wares and at once recognised the voice of her husband. She went near the gates and called the pedlar near, but he did not recognise her as her face was hidden with a veil. Before anybody could notice her, she gave two gold coins to the pedlar and told him to buy two horses and after three days to wait for her near the palace walls. Saying this she went inside the palace.

When the king returned from his hunt he went to see the girl and found her unhappy. The king asked her the reason for her annoyance. In answer to the king's question the girl said 'Your Highness, on the one hand you want to marry and make me your queen but on the other hand, I am treated like any ordinary captive without any influence of my own. This has made me sad'. On hearing this, the king at once gave her all the keys of the palace, reminding her that there were only a few days left until the wedding. The girl told him that she was aware of that.

After three days the king went hunting again. The husband had also counted the days and on the night of the third day went near the wall of the palace along with the two horses. While he was waiting for his wife, he dozed off. Just then, Baldy, the town's executioner passed by, tipsy and tottering, after a drinking bout. As he was passing, he saw two bundles rolling down from the wall and then somebody jumping down. Baldy recognised the woman. As ill luck would have it, the wife thought that Baldy was her husband and asked him to lift the bundles on to one of the horses, while she quickly mounted another and galloped off. Baldy followed close behind.

The girl looked back and saw that they had left the town far behind. She breathed a sign of relief. Slowing down her horse, she asked her husband how he was able to find her. Baldy could not answer but made a noise through his nose. This made the girl suspicious. So she stopped her horse, and looked towards the man who was riding beside her. On seeing the bald man she was greatly alarmed and cursed herself for being so careless.

But she did not lose heart and tried to think of some plan. Being an intelligent women she quickly made a plan to do away with Baldy. So she said to him, 'Listen, I had decided to marry the very first man whom I saw, after leaving the palace. Now, as luck would have it, you are the first man whom I saw. Tell me how I can marry you. You look so ugly with your bald pate. Go and find a pan of oil, so that I can cure you of your baldness. Only then will I marry you'. Hearing this from such a beautiful woman, who was not only marrying him, but was curing him of his baldness was a windfall for him. He rushed to a nearby village to buy some oil. The girl heated the oil and with a strong heart, poured it over the head of Baldy. He died instantly.

After doing away with Baldy, she rode on alone but met four hunters a little while later. The moment they saw her they started fighting among themselves. Each one of them said he wanted to marry her. Then she said to them, 'Now listen to me. It is not possible for me to marry all of you. I will tell you what to do. Give me your bows and arrows and I will shoot in four directions. The first person to bring me back an arrow can marry me'. The hunters agreed to the suggestion. The girl had strong arms and the arrows went quite a distance. When the hunters rushed off to get the arrows, the girl galloped away.

Farther on she came across four gamblers. As soon as they saw her, they forgot their gambling and began quarrelling with each other to possess her. In order to tackle the rogues she said, 'I cannot marry all of you. I will give you four bowls of wine. The person who drinks his bowl of wine in one gulp, without getting drunk, will marry me'. The gamblers agreed and gulped the wine but all became drunk. She quickly made her escape.

Now she realised that it was not possible for a woman to travel alone. All the troubles which she faced were merely because she was travelling alone. She decided to do something about it.

The girl opened one of the bundles and, took out a suit of men's clothes and changed into them. Now, she looked just like a man. That day she reached a town.

In this town she found many strange things. All the people were wearing new clothes and were carrying hunks of meat, pigeons and live chickens in their hands. They were all looking towards the sky. The girl in man's attire approached one person and asked him the reason for all the commotion. The stranger replied that the king of the town was dead and that he had a Bird of Happiness which had been released. The person on whom the bird sat would be declared the new king. As the stranger was explaining, the Bird of Happiness appeared in the sky and people got more excited. The bird circled over the heads of the crowd, and then perched itself on the shoulders of the girl who was in her man's clothes. All the people surrounded her, and respectfully asked her to enter the king's palace. Everything happened so suddenly that the girl could not make anything of it. She wanted to escape

but it was an age-old custom which could not be violated without severe punishment.

So with the will of God, she became king of a vast dominion. Even the king who wanted to marry her was under her protection. Being an intelligent person, she soon began to understand the business of the state. Her rule was so just that the people of her kingdom soon began to love their new king. They adored their king and wanted to see him happy so they wanted him to get married. She told them politely that she did not have any desire for marriage yet, but whenever she felt like marrying, she would let them know.

One day while she was busy on state affairs, a minister entered and announced: 'Your Majesty, four hunters have come and want to bring a suit against a woman who had promised to marry one of them, but then ran away. Your Highness, you will have to deal with this case, as the hunters say that the woman has come to your city'. The king ordered the minister to take the hunters into custody until the woman was found since the case could only be decided then.

After a few days, there appeared four more people to file a complaint against a woman who had tricked them with a promise of marriage. Again the king told the minister that they would be dealt with when the woman was found. After a few more days the king who had wanted to marry her and who was now under her protection, also came to meet his superior. She had to receive him with all the pomp and show that royalty required. She recognised the king whom she hated to the marrow of her bones. The king wanted to talk about some problem, but she very arrogantly told him to discuss it with her minister. After a while, the minister came and told her that the king said that he had married a woman who had run away to this country. She ordered the minister to take the king into custody until the woman was found. The minister was a little startled, but did as he was told.

After a week or so, the minister informed her that another man, who was poor and very young, had come looking for his wife. She knew that he was none other than her loving husband. She told the minister to bring him before her and saw that he was her husband, whom she loved so much that being separated from him had meant loss of sleep, appetite and peace of mind. But he did not recognise his wife who was now a king. She sent all the servants and attendants away and said, 'You are searching for your wife. Do you know if she has any special mark on her body?' The husband told her that his wife had a black mole on her right shoulder upon which she unbuttoned her robe and showed him the mark. He immediately recognised his wife, but she begged him to be discrete. She asked him to dress like a woman and to dine in the tavern. She let him go and the case was finished.

Next day, the 'king' and his ministers went strolling in the town. She suddenly stopped outside a tavern where a young woman was eating her food, and looked at her for a long time. She told her ministers, 'Gentlemen, I know you want to see me married. That woman in the tavern is the only woman whom I want to make my wife'. When the ministers heard this, they were very happy and promised to arrange the wedding without delay.

The royal wedding was a grand one. After the wedding the king taught her husband how to manage the state affairs. When she saw that her husband could really manage governing the kingdom, she told him that they could not live in disguise all their life. They had to act.

In order to reveal the whole story she summoned the ministers. Now was the time, she told her husband, to deal with the cases of the men in custody. The husband knew everything about the men whom his wife had tricked because she had told him.

According to the order of the king, the palace bell began to peal. It was a signal for the people of the town to gather before their king. The ministers also hastened back to the palace, where the townspeople were congregating. They were wondering why the king had called them there. In a few minutes the girl appeared on the high platform and told her true story to the people. The people were moved and shed tears of compassion for the brave, beautiful and intelligent woman. They said that she should pronounce a just punishment on those who had maltreated her. Then the girl said to her ministers, 'Release the four gamblers. If I had not run into them they would not have harmed me. The other four hunters should also be released, as they did not do any harm to me. As for the vicious king, he should stay in prison for his whole life or he will try to bully other women again'. With her intelligence she won the hearts of the people and both the husband and wife ruled for a long, long time.

3

Why rabbits have pink eyes and long ears

Once there was a time when all white rabbits used to have blue eyes and short ears unlike nowadays.

Long ago, there was an old mother rabbit, who had a little son. They lived in a burrow at the foot of a hill. The baby rabbit grew into a pretty white rabbit, much stronger than his mother. But as ill luck would have it, the young rabbit grew up to be very lazy and as he grew he became more lazy and arrogant. When he was a fully fledged grown-up rabbit he behaved like a baby rabbit and refused to do anything. He was not only lazy and arrogant but ill mannered too.

One night, without any reason, he shouted at his mother and told her that being a white rabbit, he would not sleep on an ordinary bed but should be provided with a snow-white bed. The poor mother rabbit had to give a new white bed to her insolent son.

One day, the old mother rabbit went out to search for food deep in the hills, while her lazy white son stayed at home as usual. There was a storm and rain and the poor mother was drenched. Still she roamed around looking for some food which she could not get. Empty-handed she went back home late in the evening. The young white rabbit was waiting for his mother, because he was hungry. When he saw her coming back empty-handed, he became very angry and abused her.

The poor old mother was very sad and said to her son, 'Child, I was wandering about looking for food the whole day and tried to avoid the storm but could not get anything. You should find your own food. For today you can have half the turnip which I have kept in the larder'. That day the white rabbit had only half a turnip to eat. At night, he kept brooding on his mother's comment that he should find his own food. What did she think about him? Couldn't he find his own food? Wasn't he capable of finding his food for himself? He said to himself, 'From now on I will show her that I can find my food; I am not going to rely on her'.

Next morning he got up and told his mother that he was going to find his own food. His mother knew that he had never been out of the house, so she asked him to go with her. But the insolent rabbit did not listen to his mother and went outside.

He ran blindly from one place to another in search of food. He searched and searched, until he became very tired, with mud splattered on his beautiful white fur. He was tired and frustrated. He was wondering why he could not find anything to eat since his mother had always brought something or the other to eat. Now he was really hungry. He saw a big shady tree, and thought of relaxing a bit, but because he felt so tired he fell asleep. After some time he was awakened by a long doleful howl. The moment he opened his sleepy eyes, he saw a huge brown wolf running towards him. Trembling with fear, he ran for his life, with the wolf close after him. Fortunately, the young rabbit had keen eyes and swift legs. He saw in front of him a little hole at the foot of a hill, and dashed towards it with all his might. The wolf began to scrape at the opening with his paws and teeth, but in vain. After some time, he gave up and went away.

The white rabbit waited until he was sure that the wolf had gone. He came out timidly and again went in search of food. By now he was dying with hunger and thirst.

He saw a pond, used by the water-buffaloes as a wallow and ran to it to quench his thirst.

The pond ws full of leeches. The white rabbit did not know anything about leeches so without looking he put his nose in the water. As he was about to drink water a big leech fastened itself firmly on to his nose. The rabbit sneezed violently. He felt a great pain at the tip of his nose and scratched it frantically. It was only with immense difficulty that he got rid of the leech. Blood began to flow from the spot where the leech had been.

He was now exhaused with hunger and fatigue. He went through the trees and came across a small tree, covered with thick clusters of ripe berries. Some squirrels and birds were fighting over them. The rabbit was overjoyed at the sight of the berries. He drove the squirrels and the birds away, and began to enjoy the berries himself. The berries were sweet and juicy, and he gobbled the lot, forgetting his weariness, the bruises on his legs, his terrifying experience with the big wolf, the leeches and even the thought of his mother which faded away from his mind. He was eating the berries and muttering to himself, 'Oh! what a heavenly place! This is the place for me'. He ate his fill, relaxed and soon was fast asleep.

Night was approaching and the air became cooler and cooler. The cold woke the rabbit from his slumber. Finding himself alone in the jungle in the dark, he took to his heels and ran for home, where his mother was waiting anxiously for him. On seeing her son back home she was very happy. She asked him, 'Oh! my child, I was worried about you. Did you get anything to eat?' The rabbit nodded morosely in reply. She asked him about the bleeding nose, which irritated the ill-mannered rabbit and he told his mother to mind her own business. The poor mother knew how bad tempered he was, so she told him to go to sleep. Next morning the mother rabbit went out in search of food as usual and the white rabbit slept till noon. When he got up, he felt hungry and went out in search of food, hoping to find something better. Suddenly, he saw a field full of ripe melons, which made his mouth water. After looking around stealthily he crept into the field and ate a lot of melons and took some more back home. When the rabbit's mother asked him where he had got them he lied and said that he got them deep in the mountains.

He enjoyed his melons in the house dreaming about the place where they grew.

Next day he went there to eat melons again. Boldly he jumped into the field and began plundering the melons. But this time, the owner of the field came and, when he saw the rabbit eating his melons, got so annoyed that he tried to hit the rabbit hard with a stick, yelling abuse. Fortunately, the blow missed, because it could have killed the white rabbit. Scared to death, the rabbit ran home and hid in a corner. He did not tell his mother, who would never have expected her son to behave as he had.

The farmer went to his house and made a big pot of paste, with sticky rice, moulded it into a scarecrow and put it in the field.

Next day, the rabbit went to the field to steal melons again, but there he saw the scarecrow. Thinking that the farmer was standing there, he took to his heels. As I said, the rabbit had a keen eye, reaching a distance. He saw that the figure was a fake, because it did not move. Emboldened, he came back and entered the field. He called for the scarecrow, but it did not move or speak. In order to be sure the rabbit went near it and hit it with his paw. Lo! he got stuck in the sticky rice paste. The more he tried to extricate himself, the more he was glued to it. Eventually, his whole body got stuck to it.

In the meantime the farmer came into the fields and saw the thief of the melons. He gave a hearty laugh at the condition of the white rabbit.

Now he realised that he had been trapped with a mass of paste and as it was difficult to escape, the rabbit pleaded with the farmer, 'Please, sir, forgive me this time. I will never steal your melons again. Please, please set me free'. The silly young rabbit was pleading so pathetically that the farmer took pity on him and decided to free him.

But to the farmer's dismay, the rabbit's whole body was embedded in the paste. Only his ears were sticking out. There was nothing for it but to pull him out by the ears. The farmer took hold of his ears and pulled with all his might. As he tugged, the young white rabbit's ears were pulled longer and longer and ever since then, rabbits have had long ears.

And what about the pink eyes? Well, the farmer wiped all the sticky paste off the rabbit's body and set him free. But he did not wipe the thin film of blood off the rabbit's eyes. Since then white rabbits have had pink eyes as well as long ears.

4

The old woman

Once upon a time, there lived an old woman in a small village. One day, as she was sweeping the floor of her house, she found a copper coin. She put it inside her little red spice jar, and noticed that the jar was half-full of rice.

Later on, she took out some rice for her breakfast leaving only one handful in the jar. At noon, when she went to the jar again, she found to her surprise, that it was still half-full. Again she took out a few handfuls for her lunch leaving one handful behind as before. Yet when she went to get rice for her evening meal, the jar was still half-full.

The old lady was very happy. She realised that it was because of the copper coin that the jar was filling with more and more rice.

In the hills close by there lived a tiger. On hearing about this copper coin, he came out of his den and went to the old woman to demand the coin. But she refused to part with it. The tiger got very angry and threatened the old woman saying that he would come back in the evening and, after devouring her, would take away the wonderful coin. Saying so he stalked off.

The poor old woman was very frightened and wept for a long time. But after a while she dried her tears, took out her sickle, and began to sharpen it.

The little dried peas heard the noise and asked her what she was doing. The old woman said, 'Oh my dear little peas, what shall I tell you? The news is not good. The tiger of the hills wants to kill me and take my copper coin. But I don't want to give him my coin. That is why I am sharpening my sickle.'

On hearing her story, the little peas wanted to help her and told her so. But the old woman asked them how they could help her. They told her that they would sleep on the floor by the door. Then they all jumped down and rolled themselves into place by the door.

An egg also asked the old woman why she was sharpening the sickle. The old woman again told her story of the wicked tiger who wanted to kill her and to take away her coin and that was why she was sharpening the sickle to kill the tiger.

The little egg wanted to help the old woman too. She asked him what he intended to do. He said he would hide himself in the ashes of the hearth.

There was a little crab, who heard the noise and asked her what she was doing. She told the crab that the tiger of the hills wanted to kill her, in order to steal the copper coin and that was why she was sharpening her sickle to kill the wicked tiger.

The crab also wanted to help her by hiding in the pitcher of water. And the little crab climbed into the pitcher while the old woman went on sharpening her sickle.

Even the big door-bar heard the noise of the sharpening of the sickle and asked the old woman what she was doing. The old woman told the big door-bar about the tiger and the copper coin. She wanted to kill the tiger and that was why she was sharpening the sickle. The big door-bar also wanted to help her and told her that he would sleep on the edge of her bed. And the big door-bar climbed on to the bed.

A frog also came, heard everything and wanted to help her by crouching at the head of her bed. And the little frog leaped up and crouched at the head of the bed.

The spinning wheel heard the swish, swish of the sickle and asked the reason. After listening, it also wanted to help the old woman by staying in one corner of the room.

A big hammer also wanted to help her, by perching on the lintel above the door. So the big hammer took its place above the door.

Night fell. The sickle was sharp and shining. The old woman went to bed, taking the sickle with her. Then, along came the tiger. Inside the house it was quiet and pitch dark. No sooner had he set foot within the threshold than the little round peas on the floor began to twist and turn and roll. Down went the tiger with a crash. he recovered himself and groped his way into the kitchen, and blew on the embers to get some light. All of a sudden, bang! The little egg living in the hearth exploded, hurling ash into his face and eyes, so that he was blinded. He went to get water to rinse his eyes, but when he dashed his paw into the pitcher, the little crab waiting there caught him with his strong pincers, and held on till the blood flowed.

The tiger, sore and furious, pulled himself away, and panting heavily, blundered along, trying to find the old woman. But when he reached the bed, the big door-bar sprang up and rained a shower of blows on him.

The little frog at the head of the bed joined in, noisily croaking and encouraging the door-bar to beat harder and harder.

Meanwhile, the spinning-wheel in the corner of the room roared and whirled.

The tiger was terrified. At that very moment, the old woman jumped out of the bed, brandishing her sickle, and the tiger turned and ran to the door. But the good little peas rolling and spinning on the ground, made him skid right across the floor until he hit the door with a crash at which the sledge hammer leaped down, and threw itself squarely on his head with a mighty thud.

Up ran the old woman, and with one stroke of her sharp sickle, killed the wicked tiger.

5

The mean farmer

Once upon a time there was a farmer who owned a garden of pear trees. These trees bore nice juicy pears which he sold in the market to earn his living.

One day he took a cart full of sweet pears to the market and hoped to get a good price for them. On reaching the market he came across a poor priest in rags with a torn cap, who demanded one pear. The peasant refused him but the priest would not go. The farmer got very angry and began to rebuke him but the priest was very adamant in his demand. He said to the peasant, 'There are several pears in your barrow. I am only asking for one.' But the farmer was very mean and refused to part even with one pear without getting its price.

Annoyed by the noise a craftsman in his shop bought one pear and gave it to the priest in order to stop the disturbance. The religious man thanked the craftsman and told everybody present that he was not mean because he had renounced the world. That is why he wanted to invite everybody to share his sweet and ripe pears. One of the people asked him why he had demanded a pear from the peasant when he had his own pears. He told him that he first needed a pip to plant the tree.

With these words he began to eat the pear, enjoying every bit of it. After finishing it, he had a pip in his hand, which he buried in a deep hole. Then he asked the people in the market for some soup to water it. A few curious people fetched some hot water from an inn and the priest poured it over the buried pip. Thousands of people gathered to see what was happening. Within moments a shoot came out before their very eyes. It grew and grew and within no time became a full grown tree, with leaves and branches. The tree blossomed and soon its fruits ripened. The priest climbed the tree and began to distribute the fruit to the people. It was only a matter of minutes before the tree was eaten bare. The priest then took his axe and cut the tree down. He lifted the tree on his shoulder and calmly walked away.

While the priest was practising his magic the farmer also came around to watch, forgetting all about his own pears. When the priest had gone he looked for his cart. The pears were gone. It was only then that he realised that the priest had distributed his pears. Even the handle of his cart had been chopped off recently. The peasant was mad with anger and ran after the priest but he was not to be found anywhere. All the people in the market place burst out laughing at him. One of them said, 'Poor peasant, just one pear cost him his whole load of juicy pears along with the handle of his cart.'

6

The pearl of honesty

A daughter was born to the dragon king of the eastern sea. The princess was a great beauty. Nature had not only given her unparalled beauty but also great intelligence. As she completed the eighteenth year of her life her father began searching for a suitable bridegroom for his beautiful and intelligent daughter. But to his dismay, none of the men he chose met with her approval.

One day, the general of the kingdom, returned from inspecting the riverside and informed the princess that there was a man answering her description. He lived on the river bend and was known far and wide for his honesty and bravery. His parents were dead but he had an elder brother with whom he was living at that time. The brothers were poor and made a living as hunters.

On hearing the general's description, the princess was very happy, but the dragon king was not pleased. First, the man was poor and secondly, he was not from a royal family. He said to his daughter, 'My good daughter, how are we to know that he is really an honest person? I don't think he is worthy of a princess like you. You should not think much about him as I don't like it'. The princess became very sad and, from then onwards neglected her appearance. The king was concerned about her and consulted his councillor about the condition of the princess. The councillor thought of a plan which the king liked immensely.

That very night, the honest man, whose name was Ah Er, dreamed that a white-haired old man came and told him that a fair maiden was waiting for him on the bank of the river and that he should propose marriage to her. Ah Er woke up and described his dream to his elder brother. However, the elder brother whose name was Ah Da was envious and told Ah Er not to take his dream seriously. He also told him to go back to sleep. Ah Da did not sleep but got up stealthily, and went to the river. In the meantime Ah Er also got up and not finding his elder brother sleeping in his bed, went to the bank of the river where Ah Da was.

The place was full of enchantment and beauty. And amid such beauty sat an extremely beautiful maiden, her long hair trailing in the river. Both Ah Da and Ah Er went up to her and asked her to marry him. The maiden, in reply, asked them, 'Who is more honest and brave?' Ah Da and Ah Er both replied together, 'I am.' On hearing this reply the maiden said, 'I want, more than anything else in the world, a luminous pearl that shines by night. Whoever can get it for me will be my husband.'

Both the brothers asked her where they could find such a pearl? The maiden told them that such a pearl was in the treasury of the dragon king of the eastern sea. Then she gave them each a water-clearing clasp to make a pathway for them in the sea.

The brothers bowed their farewells and each went his way. Neither of the brothers knew where the eastern sea was. However, they made certain arrangements and set out on a long journey.

On his way to the eastern sea the elder brother Ah Da reached a certain village, which had been destroyed by a flood. The fields were waterlogged and almost all the houses were under water. The old people and children had taken shelter on the mountainside while the young men undertook the work of rescue. In spite of all efforts, the water did not recede. This caused panic among the village folk and the wise men of the village assembled to find some solution to the problem. Then the oldest folk suggested that only the Golden Dipper could bail out water from the village. This Golden Dipper belonged to the dragon king. Now the problem was who could accomplish the task of borrowing the Golden Dipper from the dragon king. While all this discussion was going on Ah Da happened to pass by. His food was exhausted and he was thinking of replenishing his supplies, when he heard the talk of the town. He told the village folk that he was on his way to see the dragon king. He could borrow the Golden Dipper, if they provided some bread for him.

The villagers were very happy to know that he could help them. They collected all the food they had and gave it to him.

After two days Ah Er arrived at the same village. He was very concerned when he saw the condition of the place and its people. He worked with them for a whole day and when he heard about the Golden Dipper, told the people that he could borrow it from the dragon king as he was on his way to see the king. The villagers seemed somewhat puzzled, because just two days back another man had promised the same thing. However, they believed him, because he looked like an honest person. Though Ah Er had nothing to eat, he declined their offer of food. He dived and swam away. When he reached the eastern seas, he found Ah Da waiting for him, because he was afraid to dive alone in the sea. To Ah Da the sea was awesome in its vastness and the horrendous noise of the waves. He asked his younger brother to dive into the sea first. Without the slightest hesitation, Ah Er dived into the sea with the water-clearing clasp in his hand. This magic clasp made a path in the sea, and the brothers dived down to the bottom of the sea.

Soon they reached the gates of the palace of the dragon king and told the guards that they had come to see him.

The king was happy to see them and took them to his treasure house. On reaching there he said to the brothers, 'Gentlemen, you can take anything you like from here on one condition. You cannot take more than one item. All of these are priceless things and you may choose anything.'

On seeing the treasure house, Ah Da was wonder-struck. In his thoughts was the hand of the pretty maiden whom he wanted to marry. For that purpose he chose the brightest and biggest pearl. He wanted many other things but the guards ordered him to go out.

Them came Ah Er. He too saw the luminous pearls but did not touch them because he had promised to give the villagers the Golden Dipper. He picked up the Golden Dipper and came out of the treasury. The king wanted them to stay with him for some time, but they refused politely and came to the shore of the sea. Ah Da rode away on his horse leaving his brother Ah Er behind. When he reached the flooded village people came running, hoping for the Golden Dipper. The poor people were very sad, because the water had not receded, the houses were collapsing and the crops had died.

Next day Ah Er arrived at the village and shouted to the people that he had borrowed Golden Dipper from the king. The villagers were overjoyed at the sight of Ah Er.

At the first scoop with the magic dipper, the water in the houses receded. At the second, the water from the fields receded and with the third all the water on the flat land vanished. After the water had receded, there appeared a large oyster on the fields. People were amazed to see it. They opened the oyster shell and found a large black pearl in it. Since the villagers were very grateful to Ah Er for his help, they said, 'Dear stranger, because of this dreadful flood we don't have anything precious to give you in return for the help you have given us. So please keep this black pearl as a token of our gratitude'. Ah Er thanked them and put the pearl in his bag. He said goodbye and went back home. He was very happy that he had helped the people in their distress.

On the other hand, Ah Da arrived home, and with respect presented the luminous pearl to the fair maiden and pressed her to marry him without delay. But the maiden told him to wait until night because she wanted to see whether the pearl was genuine or not.

In the evening when Ah Da came to the river, he took out the pearl from his bag to see. But to his despair, he found that the pearl had lost its shine completely. He wailed in despair and threw the pearl on the ground, treading on it in desperation. The pearl broke and some foul liquid oozed from it which smelt as foul as pus.

On the third day, Ah Er arrived home and went to the maiden with bowed head and said, 'Please excuse me. I could not bring the luminous pearl to win your hand. I think I am not that lucky.' But the maiden asked him to show whatever he had brought. Ah Er told the maiden that it was an ordinary pearl, given to him as a present. Ah Da who wsa listening teased Ah Er saying that it was worse than the rocks on the river bend. But the maiden told him to wait until evening to see whether it was genuine or not.

When it ws evening, Ah Er opened his bag to take out the black pearl. It was a magnificent sight. The pearl illuminated the whole atmosphere. It was brighter than the moon. The silver light illuminated the river and made it as bright as day.

Ah Da could not open his eyes in the dazzling glare of the pearl. After some time, when he did open them he saw before him a golden palace on top of which was the luminous pearl. Ah Er and the fair maiden, hand in hand were entering the palace to get married. And that is how the king's daughter got married to the most honest and brave of men.

7

The twin-headed phoenix

Long, long ago, there lived two close friends who were of the same age. They were such good friends that whatever they did they did together, and whatever they ate, they ate together. As ill luck would have it, one of them fell seriously ill and died, leaving the other in great grief. He could not bear the shock, and soon he too fell ill and died like his friend. After the two were dead, their bodies turned into a phoenix with two heads. It had four legs, two wings, and a joint waist. So now, too, they were inseparable. Every day they looked for food or pecked at fruit in the forest together.

One day a hunter came to the forest and saw the double-headed phoenix pecking fruit on a tree top. As he was about to shoot it, he saw a strange sight. He saw that one of the bird's heads had found a ripe fruit but instead of eating it on its own shared it with the other. This happened again and again. Their affection for each other moved the hunter so deeply that he could not kill them.

The hunter went back to the town and narrated this incident to everyone. The news spread quickly. Somehow it reached the palace and the king also heard the story. After hearing this strange story the king sent his game-keeper to find the strange bird, but was not successful. However, one morning he suddenly spotted it on a tree pecking fruit. As he was about to shoot, it flew to another tree. The same thing happened when he aimed for the second time. He tried time and again, but always with the same result. As it was getting dark, he gave up and came home dejectedly.

That night, the game keeper brooded over how to catch the bird. He sat for hours thinking and thinking. Finally, he hit upon an idea. He sat up all night making slip knots, and before dawn, went to the forest and placed them on those branches which were most heavily laden with ripe fruit.

In the early morning, the twin-headed phoenix alighted on one of these branches to feed on the fruit. This time it was caught and could not fly away. That was how the bird fell into the hands of the gamekeeper, who presented it to the king. The king was very happy to see the wonderful bird. He got an exquisite cage of gold made for the bird and fed it delicious fruit, grain and sweet juice every day. Even in the cage the bird-heads continued to be affectionate towards each other and always shared their food and drink. Their deep affection for each other gave rise to great envy in the heart of the king. He wanted to separate the two heads and to make two phoenixes. He began to feed only one head, leaving the other to starve. But when the head that was being fed found that the other was getting nothing to eat, it gave up eating too. The king tried his best to force the phoenixes to eat, but without success. The king was furious. He summoned all his courtiers and issued a decree that whoever could separate the two heads and make two live phoenixes, would be given half his kingdom.

One of the courtiers came to the king and said that he would separate the two heads into two live phoenixes provided the king kept his promise. The king assured him of his promise. The courtier then said, that he would accomplish the task within a month, but he had to take the bird with him. The king agreed, so the courtier took the bird with him to his house and said he would come back after a month.

The courtier hung the cage in the back veranda of his house. Every day, he fed the bird himself with dainty grain and fruit. He watched keenly the two heads sharing their food with great affection. All the time he was thinking of how to separate them. After several days of keen observation he discovered that at a certain time the two heads would always turn away in opposite directions, which, he thought would be an opportune moment to separate them. The next day, as soon as he saw the two heads turn away from each other, he drew close to one of them and whispered some nonsense in its ear. After this he walked straight into his room again. When the other head turned back, it asked what the courtier was saying but the first head could not tell it anything. It showed its ignorance. From then on, the courtier repeated the same trick.

This began to arouse suspicion among the two heads of the phoenix. Frequent quarrels began to arise between them. At last, during one of their fiercest wrangles, in a violent fit of temper, they tore apart their joint waist. As a result the double-headed phoenix became two separate phoenixes.

Seeing the twin-headed phoenix breaking itself into two, the courtier's happiness knew no bounds. He immediately went to the palace to present them to the king and asked for his half of the kingdom. But the king was in no hurry to oblige the courtier. Every time, the courtier asked for his reward, the king would turn him away with more sweet talk. So the courtier ended up with nothing. The gamekeeper who had caught the phoenix suffered the same fate. The king gave him no reward, because this was the way the king discovered who the crafty and clever people in his court and kingdom were.

8
Bayberry

Once there lived in the mountains a woman who had a beautiful daughter whose name was Little Red. Little Red always liked to dress in red, so people gave her this unusual name.

One day as the mother and the daughter were ploughing and sowing in the fields, a gale suddenly blew up in the sky, and there appeared an evil dragon, who stretched down his claws, caught Little Red in a tight grip and flew off with her towards the west. The poor mother could not do anything to rescue her daughter. She cried uncontrollably. Red was also crying and telling her mother that her brother would rescue her. Wiping away her tears her mother gazed at the sky muttering that she did not have a son but only a little daughter.

Weeping, she staggered home and had got half way there when her hair was caught in the branches of a bayberry tree growing by the roadside. While she was disentangling her hair, she spotted a red, red berry dangling from a twig. She picked it and swallowed it without thinking.

When she arrived home, she gave birth to a boy with a round head and red cheeks. She named the little boy Bayberry.

Bayberry grew up very quickly and was a fine young lad of fourteen or fifteen years in just a few days.

The mother wanted to tell Bayberry about the dragon and Little Red, so that he could think of some way of rescuing his sister, but kept quiet, because of the fear of inflicting such a dangerous task on him. All she could do was weep to herself in secret.

One day a crow sat on the roof of Bayberry's house and sang a song depicting the story of his sister, imprisoned by the dragon who made her dig the rocks with bare hands. Bayberry asked his mother to tell him what had happened.

With tears streaming down her cheeks, his mother told him that it was true that he had a sister called Little Red, whom the evil dragon had taken away. Lots of people were killed by this dragon.

Bayberry picked up a big stick and told his mother that he was going to rescue his sister, Little Red, and kill the evil dragon.

Helplessly, his mother watched him leave with misty eyes.

For many days and nights Bayberry walked, for miles and miles. On a mountain road, he saw ahead of him, blocking the way, a large rock. It was pointed and rubbed smooth by all the travellers who had to climb it. One wrong step would mean a nasty fall. Bayberry knew that it was his first obstacle and he should remove it, otherwise it would be the undoing of many more people.

He thrust his big stick under the rock and heaved it with all his might. The stick could not take such a load and with a big crack broke in two. Then he put both his hands under the rock and tried to shift it, with all his strength. The rock rolled into the valley.

At that very moment, a shining golden reed pipe appeared in the pit where the rock had been; Bayberry picked it up and blew on it. It gave out a piercing sound which echoed for a long time and suddenly, all the earthworms, frogs and lizards by the roadside began to dance. The quicker the tune the faster the creatures danced. As soon as the music stopped, they ceased dancing. Seeing this, an idea struck Bayberry. He thought he knew how to deal with the evil dragon.

After travelling a few miles, with the golden reed pipe in his hands, he climbed a huge rocky mountain and saw a ferocious-looking dragon coiled at the entrance to a cave. Piles of human bones lay all around him. He also saw a girl in red, chiselling away at the cave. Tears were streaming down her cheeks. The evil dragon whipped the girl on the back with his tail shouting that she was ungrateful and loathsome because she refused to marry him. He also threatened to make her hew a cave in order to teach her a lesson and also warned her that she should be put to death if she failed.

Bayberry realised that the girl was none other than his sister. He could not control himself and shouted at the evil dragon, abusing him and calling him a wicked monster and evil fiend. He told the dragon that as he had tormented his sister, he would end his life merely by blowing the gold reed pipe.

Little Bayberry then began blowing the gold reed pipe. In spite of all the dragon's power and control, the music set him dancing. Little Red put her chisel down and emerged from the cave to watch. Without stopping, Bayberry blew on the pipe. The evil dragon continued to dance, squirming and writhing. The quicker the tune, the faster the evil dragon moved.

Little Red came over and wanted to speak to her brother. With a gesture of his hand, Bayberry told his sister that he could not stop the music for if he did, the evil dragon would eat them both.

Bayberry kept blowing with all his strength and the evil dragon danced with all his might to the tune of the pipe. Fire came from his eyes, steam from his nostrils, and panting breath from his mouth. Then the evil dragon

pleaded with Bayberry to stop blowing the pipe. He told him that he was stronger than him. He made a promise that he would send back his sister if he stopped blowing the pipe.

Bayberry continued blowing the pipe and walked towards a big pond. The evil dragon followed him to the bank of the pond dancing all the way. With a great splash the evil dragon fell into the pond and the water rose several feet. The evil dragon was totally exhausted. Again he begged Bayberry to stop playing the pipe and admitted again that he was much stronger than him. He would stay in the pond and torture no one.

Bayberry, abusing and calling him a wicked fiend, told him to stay at the bottom of the pond and never harm anybody again. The evil dragon nodded in acquiesance and as soon as the pipe stopped blowing, he sank to the bottom of the pond.

Bayberry took hold of his sister's hand and walked happily away. They had barely gone a short distance, when they heard the sound of water splashing in the pond. They looked in that direction and saw the evil dragon emerge from the pond. He raised his head and flew in their direction, baring his fangs and clawing the air.

On seeing him, Little Red cried and asked her brother to kill the beast and not to show any mercy. Bayberry rushed back to the pond and began to blow on his pipe once more. The evil dragon fell back into the pond and began to dance again, squirming and writhing in the water.

Bayberry stood on the bank for seven days and nights, blowing a fast tune on his pipe. Finally, the evil dragon could move no longer and floated on the surface of the water. He was dead.

The sister and brother joyfully returned home, dragging the body of the evil dragon along behind them. When the mother saw both her children coming back happily, her sad face lit up as brightly as a candle in a dark room. They peeled the dragon's skin to make a house, took out the dragon's bones to serve as pillars and beams and cut off the dragon's horn to make ploughshares. With the dragon's horn they ploughed the field quickly and had no need of oxen. In this way they ploughed many fields, sowed much grain and became very rich in a short time.

Here the story ends.

9

The water buffalo

Once there lived a hard working farmer in a small village who had a water buffalo. Every day, with his plough on his shoulder, he led his water buffalo to the field.

In the month of July there was heavy rain and because of this the mud in the field was soft and sticky. The buffalo was up to his belly in it and he had great difficulty in pulling the plough. In fact, it took him a long time to plough a little piece of land.

This made the farmer very angry and with a stick he beat him, and cursed him, screaming that he was as slow as a snail. He told the poor buffalo that he should be as strong and quick as the tiger was.

The buffalo was quite indignant and asked his master· what was so special about a tiger? He wanted to see such an animal. He challenged his master saying that if he took him to the tiger he would show him who was better.

Next morning the farmer took the water buffalo to a tiger's den. When the tiger scented the buffalo he rushed out and was about to spring upon him but the water buffalo shook his sharp horns and said quite calmly to the tiger that he had come to tell him that his teeth were blunt. He asked him to sharpen them for three days and said that he would sharpen his horns. Then they would have a duel.

With a frightening roar, the tiger agreed and went back to his den. In this den the tiger started sharpening his teeth and continued for three days. After three days, his teeth were as sharp as the edge of a razor. The water buffalo sharpened his horns only for one day, and spent two days wrapping his body with layer on layer of straw, until his whole body was covered with a thick padded armour. After that he had a good roll in the mud, so that he was covered with a fine, smooth layer of black mud and no straw could be seen.

The day of the duel arrived. The water buffalo and the tiger came to the appointed place at the appointed time. When the tiger saw the water buffalo covered all over with mud, he asked him the reason for it. The buffalo replied that it was his habit to have a mud bath several times a day when it was too hot.

The tiger examined the water buffalo from head to foot, but could not find any fault with him. He thought to himself that the water buffalo had grown fatter in the last three days and was happy that he was going to get a good and heavy meal.

When the buffalo found the tiger staring at him, he said, 'Listen, tiger, you may be able to bully pigs and sheep but you will see! You will not be able to hurt a hair on my body!'

Hearing this the tiger was furious and told the buffalo that he was ready to kill him. Now that his teeth were as sharp as a razor edge he could kill him with a single bite.

Then the buffalo told him that he would lie down on the ground and would let him bite three times. After that the buffalo would butt the tiger three times with his horns.

The tiger agreed because he thought it was an advantageous offer. He accepted it readily, sprang upon the water buffalo and started to tear and rend him. After three bites the tiger thought that the buffalo should be mortally wounded, but it was not. The tiger's teeth had only torn at the straw, leaving the water buffalo unscratched.

Now it was the buffalo's turn to strike. He got up calmly, lowered his head and butted the tiger three times in succession. At the first blow, the horns pierced the tiger's stomach; at the second, they broke the tiger's back; at the third blow, the tiger's intestines came out on the buffalo's horns, and the tiger lay dead on the ground in a pool of blood.

The farmer saw all this with his own eyes and greatly admired the wisdom and courage of his water buffalo. From that day onward he treated his water buffalo with love and tenderness, and never again abused him as a stupid animal.

Since that day, people have respected water buffaloes for their wisdom, though they may not be able to plough or pull a cart as fast as a horse nor run as fast as a deer.

10

The bragging tortoise

Once upon a time, there was a beautiful lake, near a big mountain. There lived many animals in the water and on the banks of the lake. Among those animals lived two herons, who had a little tortoise as their friend. All three of them were very good friends. They played together all day long, sunning themselves on the sand and swimming in the lake. They were very happy and did not like to be apart even for a single day.

But as ill luck would have it, that year there was a drought. In the six months from March until September not a single drop of rain fell. All the rivers and lakes dried up. Even this beautiful lake could not escape the wrath of the drought. Day by day, the water became less and less. The three friends did not know what to do and brooded and sighed all day. One day the two herons decided to fly away in order to assess the situation. Next day they flew away and saw all the animals moving towards the Heavenly Lake, a very big lake.

When they came back they told the tortoise about the migration of the other animals to the Heavenly Lake, and said that they should also shift to the big lake otherwise they could die of hunger and thirst.

On hearing this, the tortoise wept, shedding tears from his small eyes because he could neither fly, nor walk fast. There was the danger of hunters picking him up on the way if he walked slowly. He accused the herons of deserting him in the time of difficulty despite being such good friends.

The tortoise wept so pitifully that the herons, unable to hold back their own tears, did not have the heart to leave him behind. So they decided to stay back themselves for the time being. They were also positive that the rains would begin.

But the weather promised no change. The days were absolutely clear and the sun beat down mercilessly. The beautiful little lake was nearly dry. The herons now thought that they could no longer live there. The tortoise also knew that they could not survive so he pleaded with them to think of a way to take him with them too as they had been friends for such a long time.

The herons also wanted to help their friends. So they thought of a plan, but were not sure whether it would work. The tortoise was excited and asked them about their plan.

The herons told him of their plan. It was that they would hold two ends of a stick in their beaks, and he could hang on to the middle. Then they could fly carrying him between them. They asked the tortoise whether he liked the plan or not.

The little tortoise was very happy. He told them to go at once.

The herons were also very pleased, but they warned him about one thing. This was that he should not open his mouth, under any circumstances. The tortoise told them that he would be very careful, because it was his life which mattered.

That evening all three of them had their last dinner on that little beautiful lake which had been their abode for such a long time. Early next morning they said goodbye to their home. The herons held the two ends of the stick and the tortoise gripped the middle in his jaws. They flew for a long time over dark forests, glittering snow-covered mountains, temples with golden tiles and vast grasslands.

Down on the earth, some people saw this scene and commented on it saying that the tortoise was very clever because he had made the herons carry him. The herons continued their flight without paying any attention to what the people were saying. But the tortoise glowed with pride, when he heard people praising him.

After some time, a group of children who were playing down below saw the three friends and cried to the herons saying that the herons were very clever, they were carrying the tortoise so high. The herons paid no heed, but concentrated on flying. The little tortoise, however, was hurt by the children's taunts. In his heart he said, 'These children are very foolish. How silly of them to say that the herons are carrying me. I was the one who thought of this plan and they don't know which of us is the cleverer'. So with all his might he began to shout at them.

But as soon as he opened his mouth, he fell head downward and tail up, straight towards a big black stone, killing himself. And that was the end of the tortoise.

11
The frog

Many, many years ago there lived a poor couple. Somehow they were making ends meet, when they discovered that a baby was on the way. With this new development, the husband was forced to leave his house to find a living somewhere far away. Before leaving for the new place, he consoled his wife lovingly and gave her the last few silver pieces he had for the good upbringing of the newborn child. He also told his wife that in spite of their poverty, they would try to bring up their child well, so that he could help them in their old age. Giving necessary instructions to his wife the husband left the village.

After three months, the wife gave birth to a baby. It was neither a boy nor a girl, but a frog.

The poor mother was heartbroken and wept bitterly. She wailed and said, 'All our hopes for a good strong son who could help us in our old age are gone. How I am going to answer people when they ask me about the baby'.

She thought of killing the frog, but could not bring herself to do it. She wanted to rear it, but was scared of people who would be sure to sneer at her.

As she was thinking, she remembered her husband's words before he went away and decided not to kill the frog; she kept it hidden under the bed. In this way, nobody knew that she had given birth to a frog-child. Within two months the frog-child grew so big that he could no longer be kept under the bed. One day, suddenly, he spoke in a human voice.

At first, the mother did not realise that it was her frog-child who was speaking but when she looked at it, she saw that it was talking to her. The frog-child said, 'Dear mother, my father is coming back in the late evening. I am going to wait for him near the end of the road.' It was true that the husband was due to come back home that very night. When he arrived the wife asked him whether he had seen his son beside the road.

The husband asked her where his son was, because he had not seen anybody on the road except an awful looking frog, who gave him a fright. The wife unhappily told her husband that it was the frog who was their son. When the husband understood that his wife had given birth to a frog he was grieved. However, he asked his wife why she had sent the frog to meet him on the way. This was a very strange thing to do.

The wife said that it was the frog who had told her that his father was coming back that night and that he was going to meet him on the road-side.

The husband was very surprised because he was sure that nobody knew of his return. He looked pleased and asked his wife to call the frog inside as it was very cold outside. As soon as the mother opened the door, the frog came in and hopped over to his father. The husband asked him how he knew of his return and the frog answered that he knew everything that was going to happen on earth.

He told them that the enemy was preparing to invade their country; so they should take him to the king, because he wanted to save their country from this grave danger.

When the father asked him, how he would do it, as he had no weapons, no horses and no experience of fighting in a war, the frog told his father not to worry but to take him to the emperor.

The father could not refuse his frog-son so he took him to the city to seek an audience with the emperor. After two days' journey, they arrived at the capital, where they saw the imperial decree displayed. It said, 'The imperial capital is in danger. My country has been invaded. We are willing to marry the princess to the man who can drive away the enemy.' The frog stretched out his hand, tore down the decree and with one gulp swallowed it. The soldier guarding the imperial decree was greatly alarmed. He could not imagine any frog accepting such a responsible duty. However, since the frog had swallowed the decree, he had to be taken into the palace.

The king asked the frog if he had the means and ability to defeat the enemy forces. The frog replied respectfully that he could do it. Then the king asked him how many horses and men he would need but he told the king that he did not need a single man or horse. The only thing he wanted was a heap of hot, glowing embers. The king immediately ordered this. Flickering flames from the embers leaped high into the air and the heat was intense. The frog sat before the fire devouring the flames by the mouthful for three days and three nights. He ate till his belly was as big as a bladder full of fat. By now the very capital of the empire was in great danger, for the enemy was already at the walls.

After swallowing flames for three days, the frog went to the top of the city wall and judged the situation. Wherever the eyes could see there were the enemy soldiers. The king asked the frog, how he was going to drive away the massive force of the enemy.

The frog asked the king to order his troops to stop using their weapons and open the city gates. The emperor turned pale with alarm when he heard these words, and showed his apprehension.

The frog told the king that he had promised to drive the enemy away so he should be obeyed. The king was helpless and ordered his troops to do as he was told.

As soon as the gate was flung open, the invaders poured in. The frog was above them in the gate-tower and, as they passed underneath, he coolly and calmly spat fire down on them searing countless men and horses. They fled back in disorder.

The king was overjoyed when he saw that the enemy was defeated. He made the frog a general and ordered that the victory should be celebrated for several days. But he did not say anything about the princess or her marriage because he did not think of marrying his beautiful daughter to a frog.

He let it be known that the princess had refused to marry a frog and then tried to marry off his daughter quickly. Finally he ordained that her marriage should be decided by throwing the Embroidered Ball.

The news spread immediately throughout the whole country and within a few days men from far and wide came to try their luck. The capital was full of people. The frog was also present.

A pavilion was built at a great height. The emperor led the princess and her train of maids, dressed in scarlet and green, to their seats high up on the stands.

The moment came when the princess tossed the Embroidered Ball into the air. Everyone in the masses, down below in the square was eager to possess the ball. But the frog, standing on one edge, drew in a mighty breath, and sucked the ball straight to him. As was the tradition, the possessor of the Embroidered Ball was to be the imperial son-in-law but the king was still unwilling to let this happen.

So he declared that an Embroidered Ball tossed by the princess could only be caught by a human hand – no other creature could take it. It was meant only for humans, he stressed.

So the princess threw a second ball. This time it was caught by a young, strong and handsome fellow. On seeing the young man the king was overjoyed and declared him the imperial son-in-law.

The occasion was celebrated by a sumptuous feast. Readers, can you guess who that handsome young fellow was? He was none other than our hero frog, now in the guise of a young man.

After his marriage with the princess he changed into a frog again. By day he was a frog but at night he stripped of his green skin and was transformed into a fine, upstanding youth.

The princess knew this but could not keep it a secret for long and one day told her father, the king. He was startled but happy. That very night the king asked his son-in-law, why he did not discard his horrid frog skin in the day also and become a handsome young man forever.

The frog man told the king that his frog skin was priceless. In winter it gave protection against severe cold and in summer it was cool and fresh. It protected him against all odds like wind, rain and fire. He also told the king that he could live for thousands of years because of the skin.

The king was intrigued and asked if he could try on his frog skin.

The frog consented and hastily discarded his skin.

The emperor was very happy at this and took off his dragon embroidered robe and put on the frog skin. But then he could not take it off again. The frog put on the imperial robe and became the emperor. His father-in-law remained a frog forever.

Readers, this was a spell cast on the young prince by a witch and the prince could only be freed if a princess married him, and her father took the skin.

The frog-prince was a good person. He ruled his people justly and benevolently for many years.

12

In search of happiness

In the olden days, there was a very poor village in Tibet. It was poor because it had no rivers, no fertile land, no warmth or fresh flowers and no fruit trees or green grass. The land was really poor and so its people suffered from hunger and cold all year round and did not know what happiness was like. But despite this, they believed that happiness did exist somewhere in the world.

The old people of the village used to say that happiness was a beautiful bird living far, far away in the east. It was their belief that wherever the Bird of Happiness flew, happiness went with it. Every year the people of the village went high into the mountains to look for this bird, but they never saw it. The popular belief was that the Bird of Happiness was guarded by three monsters, who could kill anybody by blowing through their long beards.

Once a very intelligent boy called Genfias decided to go in search of the Bird of Happiness. On the day he was to leave his village, all the villagers, male and female came to bless him for his good cause. They told him, that they would pray to God for his success and safety.

Genfias took a path towards the east. After walking for many days, he saw a large mountain covered with snow that shone like silver. There appeared a monster with a black beard. In a crow-like voice he asked Genfias who he was and why he had come there.

The boy told him his name and the purpose of his journey. On hearing this the monster laughed at him and made fun of him, saying that he was only a child and no larger than an egg compared to his own massive size. He told him that if he wanted to find the Bird of Happiness he had to kill the queen mother, otherwise he would be punished for setting foot there. Genfias told the monster that he loved his mother dearly and so could not think of killing anybody's mother. He also told him that he could do anything he pleased.

The old monster flew into a rage. He began to blow through his beard and within no time, the smooth road became a vast talus. Every stone on it was as sharp as a knife.

After walking for the first hundred miles, the soles of the boy's boots were torn off by the stones; after the second hundred miles, his feet were cut to pieces, and after the third hundred miles, his hands were torn to shreds.

By this time, his will power was at its lowest ebb. He thought of turning back towards the village. But all of a sudden, the vision of his village folk, torn by hunger and cold, gave him a new strength. He started his journey again with renewed vigour. He knew that they would be waiting for success. He had not the heart to fail them.

Genfias fell on the ground, but did not stop. He began to crawl forward. His clothes, knees and shoulders were torn. Finally he reached the end of his journey and there he found another monster, with a brown beard and a voice like the whistling wind, waiting for him.

He too asked the boy how he dared to come there. The boy told him the purpose of his coming. In his whistling sounds the monster told him that he had to kill old Grandpa. Only then could he find the Bird of Happiness.

Looking directly at the monster, without any fear, he told him that he loved his Grandpa and that was why he could never dream of harming another man's grandfather.

In his rage, the monster told him that he would starve him to death. In a fury he blew through his long brown beard and the bread bag of the boy disappeared in to the sky. Before his very eyes, the blue mountains and green rivers were turned into a boundless desert with not a scrap of food in sight.

Genfias did not bother and continued his journey. After the first hundred miles his stomach began rumbling with hunger; after the second hundred miles, he was so hungry that his head swam and he began to see stars; after the third hundred there was a sharp pain in his guts, as if they were being cut by a knife. Genfias went to a river, drank plenty of cold water and continued on his way. By the time he reached his journey's end he was nothing but skin and bones.

Now he faced another monster with a white beard. In his thunderous voice he asked Genfias who he was? Very politely but firmly the boy told him that his name was Genfias and he had come in search of the Bird of Happiness.

The monster told him that he had to present him with the eyeballs of Baima who was a maiden of great beauty. If he failed to do so, the monster would gouge out the eyeballs of the boy. But Genfias was not a coward. He told the monster that he would not even think of doing such a thing to a pretty girl.

The monster with the white beard screamed with rage. He blew through his long white beard and Genfia's eyeballs jumped out of their sockets and the poor boy became blind.

This did not stop Genfias from continuing his journey in search of the Bird of Happiness. He kept crawling towards the direction of the rising sun, and completed the journey of another nine hundred miles. He climbed a peak of a snow-covered mountain, and there he heard the voice of the Bird of Happiness.

Very tenderly, the bird asked the boy whether he had come to meet him.

Genfias was overwhelmed with joy when he heard the voice. He told him that his village folks longed day and night to see him. That was why he had come and wanted him to visit his village.

The Bird of Happiness caressed Genfias gently with his wings and sang for him. His eyeballs flew back to their sockets and now he could see even better than before. All his wounds healed and he became much stronger than before. The Bird of Happiness gave him some nice things to eat and then bore him back towards his home village. They landed on a mountain top.

Now the Bird of Happiness asked him, 'What do you want now?'

Genfias replied that he wanted happiness and prosperity for his village people. He told him that they wanted warmth and happiness, forests and flowers, fields and rivers.

Standing on the mountain top the Bird of Happiness gave three loud cries. At the first cry, the golden sun broke through the clouds and a warm breeze came down from the sky. At the second cry, dense forests appeared all over the mountains with fruit trees everywhere to be seen along with singing birds. At the third cry, green fields and rivers came into view and beautiful little animals danced merrily on the green grass.

From that very day, the people of that village were always happy and never suffered hardship again.

13

The spirit

At the foot of the Horse Mountain was a small village. In this village lived a farmer who made his living by selling grain from his fields. Every five days he would go to the small market town to sell his grain. This market was about a mile away and separated from the village by a rocky ridge.

One day he was returning from the market slightly drunk. He was riding on his mule and had just reached the rocky ridge when he had a horrid vision. At first he thought perhaps it was his imagination. But then he came down from the mule and looked keenly. Yes it was there. He saw a monster. Its huge face was blue and its eyes started from its head like those of a crab. They flashed with an angry and mean gleam. Its big mouth ran from one ear to the other like a dish full of blood. In it was a thick tangle of teeth two or three inches long. The monster was lurking by the stream where it had just stooped to drink. The farmer could clearly hear the water slurp down its throat.

The farmer was scared to death. Luckily, the monster had not seen him. Quickly, he changed his route. This was a flat path but somewhat longer than the hilly one. This road was taken by the villagers whenever they had wheelbarrows to push. The peasant rode his mule and made it run as fast as it could carry him.

As he was about to turn the corner he heard a voice calling out behind him. The voice asked him to wait. He turned to see who was calling him. He stopped and waited. It was his neighbour's son. The young boy told him that old Li was seriously ill and would not survive much longer. Old Li's son had asked him to go to the market to order a coffin. He also told him that he was coming back from the market after placing the order for the coffin. The farmer knew that old Li had been sick for quite some time, so he believed him.

The neighbour's boy asked him why he had taken the longer route when usually he took the shorter one.

The peasant felt uneasy. He wanted to avoid the question, but the boy insisted on the reason for his taking a longer route. There upon the peasant told him that he had to go to the mountain that day but seeing an ugly and horrid monster, had abruptly changed his course.

On hearing this the neighbour's boy said that the very thought was horrifying and he was scared – could he sit on the back of his mule too? The farmer consented and the neighbour's boy sat behind him on his mule.

After going a short distance the neighbour's boy asked him to describe the monster. The farmer told him that he was too upset to tell him anything then, but on reaching home he would tell him every detail.

Then the neighbour's boy replied that if he did not like to talk about it, couldn't he just look at him and tell him whether he resembled the monster. The farmer scolded him for such a wicked joke and told him that a man could never be a devil.

But in spite of the peasant's reprimanding him, the boy insisted on his looking at him. To make it more effective he tightly gripped the peasant's arm. So the farmer turned and looked at him, and true enough, there was the monster he had seen by the stream sitting behind him on his mule. In his fright he fell off the mule and remained lying on the spot unconscious.

The mule knew its way and got back home. The people of the village became alarmed and suspecting the worst, went along different paths to look for him. They found him at the foot of the rocky slope and carried him home. For three days he had very high temperature. It was only on the fourth day that he recovered consciousness and could tell them what had happened to him.

Everybody knew it was the spirit of Horse Mountain. It would always frighten the villagers in a morbid way but never harmed them seriously.

14

The unsatisfied mason

In olden times, there lived a stonemason. He was famous for his extraordinary skill at his trade.

One day a rich man wanted some stone-cutting done in his house, so he called him. On reaching the rich man's house, he saw that he lived in a spacious mansion, and was dressed in silks. He enjoyed all the delicacies from the sea and the mountains. There were many maids and servants who waited upon him. The stone mason was so envious that he gave up his work and decided to live only as a rich man.

A good-hearted fairy heard his desire and made him a rich man. The mason was overjoyed at his change of fortune.

After some time, a high ranking official went out on a tour of inspection in his sedan-chair carried by his men. Wherever he went, there was great pomp and show. People bowed and made way for the procession but when it passed by the mason's door he refused to bow before the official.

He told them that since he was a rich man and had many maids and servants he was superior to the officer. Such impertinence was not tolerated by the officer who ordered the mason's arrest. Later the mason was beaten and fined by the officer.

Wincing with pain, he got up. It slowly dawned on him that high-ranking officials were more powerful than the rich. He left everything and swore to become a great official. Again the fairy heard his desire and made him a great official. He was deliciously happy at the change.

The mason maltreated the people of his district because he could not forget the humiliation he had suffered at the hands of an official. This attitude made all the people hate him.

One day he and his henchmen, went to a hillside for inspection, where he saw a group of pretty young girls. he and his men tried to violate the honour of the maidens. The girls screamed and called out, and within no time a large crowd of Zhuang people rushed up from all sides, bearing swords, axes and hoes. They caught hold of the mason and his men and gave them a sound beating.

After the rough treatment from the people for his evil-doing, the mason thought that the Zhuang people were the bravest among the brave and decided that he would like to change back into a Zhuang. Once again, the fairy granted his heart's desire and this gave him great happiness and satisfaction.

Every day he went to the hillside with his people, to the fields and worked from morning until evening. It was very hot. The sun scorched his back while he worked. It was really difficult to bear the sun in the open. In such heat even the birds and wild beasts did not emerge from their hideouts in the day time. Water buffaloes buried themselves up to the neck in muddy water and only the glistening green rice shoots stood unyielding like the Zhuang people. The mason came to the conclusion that the sun must be the ruling force in the universe and dreamt of becoming a sun himself.

The fairy, however again granted his desire and made him the sun in the sky. Contendedly, he sent forth scorching rays of heat on the earth.

Then one day a thick black cloud hid the sun from the earth. On seeing it he said to himself, 'I never thought that a black cloud was much more powerful than the sun. How good it will be if I become a thick black cloud.'

Again the fairy satisfied him by turning him into a thick black cloud.

But a fierce wind arose and blew the cloud into pieces. The mason lamented that he did not know that the wind was much more powerful than the cloud. He prayed that he should be made a fierce wind.

Again the fairy helped and made him into a gale. He blew like a typhoon, uprooting trees and tearing down houses. There were always terrific storms.

One day it so happened that he was stopped by a huge rock. He tried his best but the rock was unmoved. He told himself that the fierce gale could not do anything to a rock. How good it would be if he was ever made a rock!

The fairy obliged, by turning him into a great rock on top of a high mountain. He was immensely satisfied by his position and thought that nobody could bully him.

After some time, however, there came a group of masons to the peak where he lay. They looked at the rock, considered it useful material, and began cutting it. The mason was frightened beyond reason.

Terrified he prayed to the fairy for help. The fairy thought that he was fit to be a mason and nothing else. So the mason was again a mason.

From that very day he worked with great devotion he never knew before. He never coveted anyone else's position or qualities and instead he became even better at his trade. Every day his clientele increased. With the passage of time, he became very famous as an incomparable mason and was held in high respect by everybody in his homeland.

15
The golden vase

Once upon a time there lived two very good friends in a small village. One day they went up to the hills to find some edible roots. They chose a spot to dig the ground. When they were digging they came across a shiny vase of gold. One of them wanted to keep it for himself but the other who was a very kind and good hearted man, wanted to share it and distribute his share among the poor.

The man who wanted to have the vase, told his friend that it was possible that the vase was not of gold because if it was so it could not have remained buried like an ordinary thing.

The good hearted friend told him that they should take it to be tested.

They came down from the hills and both stayed in the greedy one's house. In the evening while they were eating their meal the greedy man asked his friend if it was possible for him to keep the vase a while and get it tested. He promised that if it was pure then both of them could share the value.

His friend trusted him completely and agreed. The next day he went to his own home, and after several days went back to his friend's house. The moment he entered his house, he realised that something was amiss. His friend was looking very sad and gloomy. Naturally he asked the reason. The greedy one replied that he was feeling sad because of the vase. It was not of gold but was made of useless cheap tin. He also told him that they had wasted their time and energy over a fake thing.

The honest man was a bit sorry that his friend did not even show him the melted tin of the vase but he remained quite calm and tried to console his friend by telling him that they did not spend anything on it. So there was nothing to be sad about.

The mercenary friend was greatly relieved to find that the other one believed him so readily. He was jubilant that the vase was all his and that he did not have to share it with anybody.

Happily he told his wife to prepare a special meal with good wine for his friend.

Next morning before leaving, the good hearted man invited the greedy one's children to visit his house, which was among beautiful hills mountains, rivers, streams, groves and meadows with fruit trees and flowers.

The greedy one was so delighted at the thought of possessing the vase that he would have agreed to anything. He nodded his head at once and said, 'My dear brother, my children are your children. I am very pleased that you have taken the trouble to invite them to your house. Of course, I shall be glad to let them go.'

So the good hearted man took his friend's children home with him. On the way they had to pass a place where many monkeys lived so he caught two for the children. The children were overjoyed. They took them home and taught them all sorts of tricks such as dancing to music and answering commands. Each child named his monkey by his own name.

After three months the good hearted man sent a message to his friend, asking him to come and take his children back. On the day he expected him, he sent the children off to pick fruit on the hills. When his friend came, he appeared very sad and told him that he was ashamed to meet him.

The mercenary friend became concerned and asked his friend the reason for his sorrow. The honest man told him that it was so bad that he could not find the words to tell him.

The greedy one consoled him telling him that he would share the sorrow with him because they were like brothers.

Then the honest man spoke as if he was in great pain. Slowly he told the greedy one that when the children came to his house they were perfectly well. They were very happy and good, but suddenly one day they turned into monkeys. Now they only knew how to skip from one tree to another. They were not children anymore.

He stopped, and then called the children's names. Down came the monkeys at once. They climbed all over him and being very tame, climbed over the visitor as well.

His friend was greatly taken aback, and did not know what to think. He stared at the monkeys for a long while and then slowly understood. Sheepishly he said to his good hearted friend, 'Dear brother, I confess it all.

The vase is of pure gold. It has not been melted. Give me back my children, and I will share the golden vase equally with you'.

The honest man smiled and went to the hills to call the children back. Next day his selfish friend took him to his house and they shared the proceeds of the golden vase equally.

16
The black spot

Once upon a time there lived a poor man. One day he was digging the ground on the slope of the mountain, when a witch saw him and wanted to eat him. She sat on a stone staring at him. The man was busy in his work but when he looked up he saw the witch. He knew that she wanted to eat him so he said to her, 'Please don't eat me today, because I have grown weak doing this hard work. At home I have a fat hen. You can have me after I have eaten the hen and have become chubby.'

The witch agreed. In the evening, the man killed his hen, ate it, and kept a large piece for witch. Next day, he took the piece of meat to the witch and gave it to her.

The witch ate the meat but wanted to eat the man. The man said, 'It will be better if you do not eat me today. I have a fat pig at home. You can eat me when I have eaten him and become even fatter'. The witch agreed again because she believed him.

That evening the man killed and ate the fat pig and kept a chunk of pork for the witch. Next morning, he gave the witch the chunk of pork. After eating the pork she told him that since she was full she would eat him the next day.

That day the man went home and searched everywhere but could find nothing more to eat. In despair he went to his neighbours and told them how the witch wanted to eat him, and how he had saved himself; first by offering a piece of chicken and second by offering a chunk of pork. Now he said there was nothing in the house to eat and offer her. Next day she would definitely eat him. He also requested the neighbours to look after his wife and children.

The neighbours consoled him and began to think of a plan to kill the witch next day. Eventually, they thought of a plan together and promised to meet on the mountain slope the following day.

The next morning the man came to dig the ground on the mountain slope as usual. The witch was already waiting for him. As she was afraid to be seen, she had transformed herself into a tree stump and sat in front of the man in that guise. When the neighbours arrived and saw the stump, they asked the man what was in front of him.

The witch heard them and asked the man to tell them that it was a tree stump.

The man copied the witch's tone of voice and said the same. But the witch immediately corrected him and told him to speak in his own voice.

The man again repeated what the witch said.

The neighbours heard this and asked the man the meaning of his words and also told him that they did not believe what he was saying. If that object was a tree stump, he should chop it with his hoe to prove it.

When the witch heard this she cried and said, 'Just pretend that you have chopped the stump. Please be careful with my black spot. Don't touch it. It will harm me'.

The man told the witch that he would be very careful if she could tell him where her black spot was.

'It is here', she said, 'Please don't do anything to my black spot even by mistake.' The man told her not to worry as he was very careful.

He raised his hoe high above his head and brought it down with all his might on the witch's black spot. The witch died instantly and the poor man was vindicated.

17

The stealing of Rose-Red

This is a story of skilled swordsmen of China, between the late sixth and early seventh century A.D. There were three types of skilled swordsmen. The first were the sword-saints. These could change their shape at will and their swords struck like lightning. Before people knew what had happened to them their heads were rolling on the ground. However, these were high minded men who did not readily get involved in worldly business. The second were the sword-heroes. They would kill the unjust and help the oppressed. They carried a dagger concealed at the waist and slung a leather satchel over their shoulder. By means of magic, they could transform human heads into water. They could fly over the roofs and walk up and down walls, and disappear without a trace. The third kind were the murderers, who could be hired by anyone wanting to be avenged upon his enemies; to them death was an every day occurrence.

Old Dragonbeard was a swordsman of great repute and could be classified between the first and the second categories. But Molo, who is the protagonist of this story was one of the sword heroes.

At that time there lived a young man called Tai. His father was a high official and the friend of a prince. One day his father sent him to visit a sick friend. The son was young and handsome and highly gifted. As he entered the house, he was welcomed by three beautiful young slave girls. He was entertained by them and was offered all manner of delicacies. When he had eaten he took his leave, and his noble host commanded one of the slave girls, called Rose-Red to accompany him to the gate. The young man turned his head again and again to look at the beautiful slave girl. He tried not to make it obvious but the girl was so charming and attractive that he could not help looking at her. She smiled at him under her lashes and made signs to him with her hand. First she stretched out three fingers, then she turned her hand three times and finally she pointed to a little mirror which she wore on her chest. As they parted she whispered to him that he should not forget her.

When he reached home his mind and thoughts were in turmoil. He sat there absent-minded. He did not know what he wanted. He was a bit confused.

He had an old servant called Molo, who was an exceptional man. He could not see his master in such a state and very politely asked him the reason for his sadness. He begged his master to confide in him.

The young man told Molo everything about the girl and the secret signs which she had made.

Molo told his master the meanings of her signs. For instance the meaning of three straight fingers was that she lived in the third courtyard. Her turning her hand three times signified the number three times five fingers which made fifteen. And by pointing to her little mirror she meant on the fifteenth, when the moon was as round as a mirror at midnight, he was to go to her. These words cleared the confusion in which the young man had found himself. He could hardly contain himself with joy. But again he became sad thinking about how it was possible for him to go there.

Molo told him not to worry as he had already thought of a plan. He planned to buy two lengths of dark silk to veil themselves in and then to carry the young man over there. However, he knew that there was a fierce dog guarding the courtyard of the slave girl, and that this dog was as strong as a tiger and as watchful as the god. No one could pass by it. He decided to kill it. He told his master that except for him no one on earth could kill that dog.

The young master was very pleased with his servant and gave him the choicest wine and meat in return. On the appointed day, the old servant took a sledge-hammer and was gone in an instant.

Before it was supper time, he came back and said to his master, 'My Lord, the fierce dog is dead and there is no obstacle left.'

At midnight the two wrapped themselves in dark silk and the old servant carried his young master over the high wall which surrounded the palace. They approached the third courtyard, and found it deserted with the gate ajar. They saw the gleam of a small lamp and heard Rose-Red sighing deeply. The young man lifted the curtain and entered. Rose-Red leapt up happily from her couch and caught him by the hand.

She told him that she was sure he would come to see her. She complimented him for understanding her sign language and penetrating the palace. The young man told her everything that Molo had done for him.

She invited Molo in and gave him some wine and meat. She confided in Molo and told him that she was from a good family which lived very far from there. She also told him that she was kept as a slave in the house under duress. Though she had everything, such as golden goblets for drinking wine, velvet and silken clothes to wear and the most expensive jewellery to decorate herself with, she felt they were like fetters and chains for her and she wanted to escape. She requested Molo to free her from this misery with his exceptional magical powers. In return, she promised to serve his master as a slave and would never forget his good deed as long as she lived.

When the young man asked Molo, he said that he was ready to help the girl. First of all, he packed all her dowry in bags and sacks. Three times he came and left again before he had finished and then he took his master and Rose-Red upon his back and with them flew over the high walls. Nobody, not even the watchmen in the prince's castle noticed anything. On reaching home the young man concealed Rose-Red in the remotest room.

In the morning the prince discovered the disappearance of Rose-Red and the death of his fierce dog. By the execution of the theft, the prince was convinced that it was done by a sword hero. Then he gave strict orders to keep the theft a secret and to have the matter investigated secretly.

Two years passed and the young man no longer thought there was any danger. One day Rose-Red rode out of the city to the river in a light carriage. She was seen by one of the prince's servants. He reported this to his master who summoned the young man. The young man told him everything beginning with his visit to the prince's palace.

The prince made it clear to him that it was not his fault and that only Rose-Red was to be blamed, but as now she was his wife he would pardon her. The prince was very angry with Molo and wanted to punish him for this.

Thereupon he ordered a hundred armed soldiers to surround the young man's house with arrows and swords and to seize Molo at all costs. Molo took his sword and flew up to the top of the highest wall. He looked around like a hawk. The arrows came at him as thick as rain, but none struck him, and in a moment he had disappeared. No one knew where he had gone.

More than ten years later one of his master's servants came across him in the south selling medicines. He looked exactly the same as before. The lapse of ten years had not touched his strength or his looks.

18
The little camel

Once there lived a very wealthy man. He had a very beautiful daughter who was betrothed to the son of a high official. Being a rich man, he wanted to give a handsome dowry to his only daughter. One hundred white camels were included in the dowry. Among these hundred camels was a little camel who had just been weaned and was taken from his dam to make up the hundred needed for the dowry.

The mother camel missed her little one. The little camel missed her even more and ran away to try to find her.

He stumbled through the thorns and ran through the reeds, sometimes stopping to prick up his ears and listen.

The poor little thing dreamt of sleeping beside his mother. He was constantly thinking about her. He wanted to see his mother's eyes, which he thought were like the sun and the moon. He could still taste her milk which was the tastiest thing he had ever known.

While he was thinking about his mother, he came to a huge lake, which was too big for him to cross. He stood there, not knowing what to do, when a huge fish stuck its head out of the lake. It took pity on the little camel and carried him across. At the other side of the lake the little camel felt happier. But as bad luck would have it he was caught by a herdsman and tied to the neck of a male camel.

The little camel missed his mother so much that he kept crying. When the male camel realised that the little camel had been separated from his mother, he felt sorry for the

little on. In order to set him free he gnawed through the rope and set him free.

The little camel ran away as soon as he got free and was lucky enough to reach the place where he had lived before. At last he found his mother.

The mother had missed her little one so much that she was dying. She lay on the grass, weeping. On seeing her little one coming back, she was overjoyed and heaved a sigh of relief, but her end was certain. So she called her child and said, 'My dear little son, your separation has almost killed me. Though you have come back I cannot survive. Listen carefully. Stay here beside me for three days after I am dead. You will see three blades of grass growing on my head. You must bite them into three parts and eat them. Then go towards the north to look for your brother. You will recognise him by his size – he is small – and by the white hair on his neck which is especially long. Stay with him and you will live in safety. And remember, on your way to look for your brother, you must not sleep on mounds, nor should you sleep at places where men have been camping. Sleep on the south sides of slopes. When you find your brother, do what he does and walk in the middle of the caravan ...'

The mother camel died with tears in her eyes. After three nights, three blades of grass grew out of her head. The little camel ate them and went in search of his brother.

Like any other child, the little camel was full of curiosity, and wanted to sleep on a mound. But when he tried it, he found it draughty and cold. He thought about his mother's words and said to himself, 'Mother was right, it is really uncomfortable here'.

Being curious he thought of sleeping where the men were camping. That night he could not sleep well because of the noise made by other animals.

The third night he did what his mother had told him and slept on the south side of a slope. He had a very peaceful night there and he did not feel cold nor was he disturbed by other animals.

On the fourth day he found his brother.

He was still curious and wanted to have his own way. He decided not to follow his brother and not to act according to his mother's warnings.

He tried walking at the head of the caravan on purpose. But the big camel leading the caravan bit his hind legs.

Then he tried walking at the side of the caravan but was blinded by the kicked up sand.

Now he decided to walk at the rear, but the shepherd girl beat him.

By this time he had enough of his own ways and decided to stay close to his brother and to walk in the middle. Everything changed immediately. His brother looked after him well and provided the best grass and enough water to drink as well as good protection. Altogether life was very happy.

'Everything mother said was perfectly true', thought the little camel.

19

The shade of the mulberry tree

Once upon a time there lived a very rich and greedy man in a village in China. He built a huge mansion, by the side of the road, in which he lived. Right outside his house was a tall, stately mulberry tree. In summer, he would sit in the cool shade of the tree, enjoying it immensely. He was very possessive about the tree and forbade passersby the use of the shady tree.

One hot summer day when the rich man came out of the house to enjoy the cool shade of the tree, he saw a poor man resting under it. The rich man became very angry and ordered the poor man to go away.

The poor man told him that he wanted to rest for a little while under the tree, and there was no reason why he should not.

The rich man said that the tree belonged to him and so its shade was also his.

The poor man thought for some time and then told him that he wanted to buy the shade of the tree, if the rich man was interested in some money.

Since the rich man was very greedy, he was delighted to hear about the money. So, he got ready to sell the shade of the tree. After three or four middlemen agreed on a price, the shade was sold.

Every day after that, the poor man would go and rest in his shade. Wherever the shade happened to be, the poor man followed it, whether it was in the courtyard, kitchen or the sitting room of the house. From morning till evening he followed the shade and walked into rich man's house without any hesitation. Sometimes, he rested in the shade by himself, but quite often he would invite his acquaintances, with their mules or other animals to come into the shade too, and rest.

As was anticipated, a day came when the rich man could not tolerate the poor man entering his house. He scolded him and told him not to enter his house in future.

But the poor man had a ready made answer to the rich man's scoldings. He told him bluntly that he would definitely enter his house when the shade was there as he had paid for it and it was his right. The rich man was very angry when he heard this. But there was nothing he could do. After all, he had sold the shade.

One day when the rich man was entertaining his important and rich guests in his sitting room, the poor man strode in and sat down in the shade, which was now in the sitting room. The guests thought it rather unusual. But when they learned that the rich man had sold the shade, they had a good long laugh. They joked about his greed and commented sarcastically on his sale of the shade.

This was too much for the rich man. He could not tolerate it any more and so moved away to another village.

The poor man came and lived in the house and hitched his mule in the stable of the rich man. From that day anyone who happened to rest under the shade of the mulberry tree by the road was unmolested. The poor man had taught a good lesson to the greedy rich man.

20
The wise man

Many years ago, there lived an old man who had an only son. The old man was very clever and widely experienced. His main aim was to make his son as worldly-wise and experienced as he himself was. One day the old man called his son and asked him to remember three things in his life. These three pieces of advice were: 'Never make friends with a man you cannot trust. Never borrow money from a newly rich man and never tell your secrets to a soul, even your own wife.'

As usual, the old man's son keenly listened to the advice given by his father and decided to test it out. He made friends with a man he knew to be untrustworthy and borrowed money from a man who had just become rich. Then, he secretly killed a goat, stained his clothes with its blood and told his wife to wash the blood from his clothes. He made a point of telling his wife that he had killed a man and that she should keep it a secret. The wife assured him that she could never betray him.

One day, not long after, he quarrelled with his wife for some reason or the other. His wife then went to the king and told him about the murder which her husband had committed. The king immediately gave orders for the man to be brought before him.

When he was going to the palace, the old man's son requested his newly acquired friend to testify for him. But the new friend excused himself by saying that he was too busy to testify for him. Then on the way, by chance he met the newly rich man, from whom he had borrowed money. The rich man asked the old man's son where he was going. The old man's son told him everything. The rich man thought about his money and proceeded at once to squeeze money out of the young man.

When the young man was produced before the king, he bowed his head and told the king the whole story, beginning from his father's words of wisdom. The king was greatly amazed. He was full of admiration for both the old man and his son. The king dismissed the charge. But he became somewhat uneasy. He thought that the father and son were much wiser than him. They were clever and experienced. There was every possibility of their usurping his throne. These were the thoughts which gripped the king and he decided to do away with them. He gave orders for them to be buried alive.

One day, not long after this episode, the king had a terrible accident. While he was eating his meal, a little piece of bone got stuck in his gullet. All the famous doctors in the country were called to examine him but to no avail: none of them could remove the bone. The courtiers became disheartened and told the king that the old man and his son could have helped him if he had not buried them alive.

The king had completely forgotten about them. He ordered his soldiers, 'Please hurry up, go there at once, dig them up and bring them here. God willing, they may be still alive.'

When the hole was dug open, the father and son were still breathing. They had survived on a bag of dried yoghurt which the old man had hidden when they were buried. When they were told about the king's trouble, they refused to go and help him. The king again sent his courtiers, promising to give his crown and everything else if they could remove the bone and save his life.

Finally, the old man and his son agreed to help the king. They went to the king, and the old man said, 'Your Highness, in order to save your life you have to sacrifice the life of the prince, your only son.'

The king was very reluctant to do this. The time was running short and the courtiers wanted to save the life of their king at any cost. So they persuaded the king, who had to agree.

He was trembling with fear when the prince was brought for sacrifice. The old man held a sharp gleaming knife in his hand and was about to strike, when he observed the expression of fear and distress on the king's face. He ordered that a curtain should be put in front of the king so that he could not see. The king forced himself to hold his breath and listened in great apprehension. Suddenly he heard a shriek of death. He himself let out a great wail and to his amazement the wail caused his throat to move and the little piece of bone lodged there was shaken out.

Afterwards, the wise old man informed the king that this was only a drama enacted to give him a shock. The victim was not the prince but a goat. The king was extremely happy. Keeping his promise he handed over his crown and property to the old man. But the old man thanked the king and asked him to rule the country wisely and justly. The king then requested the old man to remain with him as his royal adviser. The old man consented gladly.

21
A bird with nine heads

Long, long ago, there lived a king and a queen who ruled over China for a long time. A daughter was born to them whom they loved dearly. One day the princess was walking in the garden, when a tremendous storm suddenly arose and carried her away. This was not a natural storm, but had come from the Nine-Headed Bird. The bird carried off the princess and took her to its cave. The king could not find out where his daughter had vanished to. He loved his daughter so much that when she disappeared he became very sad and listless. His advisers asked him to issue a proclamation and he ordered one to be read throughout the land: 'Whoever brings me back my daughter, shall have her for his wife.'

A young man from a neighbouring village had seen the bird carrying the king's daughter to its cave. But no one could reach the cave because it was half way up a steep rock face. No one could climb up to it from the bottom or descend to it from the top. The young man felt helpless and paced around the rock thinking. After some time another man came along and asked him what he was doing. The young man told him that the Nine-Headed Bird had carried off the princess and taken her to the cave in the mountain. The other man knew how to reach the cave. He called his friends and together, they let the young man down to the cave in a basket. As he entered the cave he saw the king's daughter sitting there nursing the Nine-Headed Bird's wound.

The Hound of Heaven had bitten off the bird's tenth head and the wound was still bleeding. The king's daughter, however, saw the young man entering the cave and told him to hide. This he did. The princess nursed the bird so well that while she was nursing its wounds all the nine heads fell asleep one after the other. Then the young man came out from his hiding place and with one sword cut off all the bird's heads. He led the princess outside and wanted her to be raised in the basket, but the king's daughter insisted that the young man must go first. The man told her that it was not safe for her to stay back. Reluctantly, the princess stepped into the basket. Before doing so, however, she took a long hairpin and broke it into two, giving one half to the young man and keeping the other herself. She also divided her silken kerchief with him and bade him guard both things carefully.

But when the other man had hauled the king's daughter up to the top he took her with him and left the young man in the cave in spite of all the poor fellow's pleading.

The young man did not lose heart. He inspected the cave carefully in case there was a way out. He saw a great many maidens who had been carried off by the Nine-Headed Bird and had died there of hunger. There was a fish pinned on the wall of the cave. When he touched it, the fish changed into a handsome young man who thanked him for rescuing him. The two young men pledge lifelong brotherhood to each other.

Very soon the young man of our story felt the pangs of hunger. He went outside the cave to find something to eat but all he could see was stones. Suddenly he caught sight of a great dragon licking a stone. The young man also licked the stone and soon his hunger was gone. He then ventured to ask the dragon how he could escape from the cave. The dragon listened and then motioned him to sit on his tail. The young man sat on the dragon's tail and in a trice was down on the ground. The dragon disappeared. He walked along the road and found a tortoise shell full of beautiful pearls. These pearls were not only priceless stones but pearls with magic powers. If they were thrown into a fire the fire stopped burning, if they were cast on the water the water parted so one could walk through it. The young man took the pearls from the shell and put them in his pocket. After some time he came to the edge of the great sea. He flung in one pearl. The sea parted and he caught sight of the sea dragon. The dragon was furious at the disturbance. Loudly, the young man told the dragon about the magic pearls with which he had been able to divide the sea.

Then the dragon invited the young man to the bed of the sea. Soon he realised that this was the same cave. The young man to whom he had pledged brotherhood was also there. He was the dragon's son.

The dragon thanked the young man for saving his son in the cave and said, 'You saved my only son and pledged brotherhood so I shall be your father. Come son, let us wine and dine for a bright future for the three of us'.

And so he lived with the old dragon and his son. One day the dragon's son told the young man that his father wanted to reward him for saving his life. He said, 'Brother, don't accept any money, nor any precious stones which my father is going to try to give you as a reward. Simply ask for the pumpkin flask which will fulfil any wish of yours.'

After some days, the dragon asked the young man what he would like to have as a reward. As planned, the young man asked for the pumpkin flask.

At first the dragon hesitated to give it but then parted with his most prized possession, the pumpkin flask.

After taking the flask, the young man left the dragon's castle. When he reached dry land, he felt hungry. It was only a matter of thinking about food and a table stood before him laden with the most sumptuous delicacies.

The young man ate and drank his fill. He had gone on for a while when he felt tired. At once a horse stood before him and he climbed on its back. When he had ridden for a little while, he thought that the horse had become too bumpy for him. At once a carriage appeared and he stepped inside. But he found the carriage jolting too much and thought about a sedan chair. And at once a sedan chair appeared before him and the young man got inside and the bearers took him all the way to the city where the king, the queen and their daughter lived.

On the other hand, the other man who had deceived the young man, brought the princess to the king and as promised, preparations were made for their wedding. But the king's daughter had no wish to marry him and told the king that he was not her rescuer. For a long time, however, the other young man failed to appear. So the imposter pressed the king, who grew impatient and announced the wedding for the next day.

Sadly, the king's daughter walked through the streets of the city, searching for the man who had saved her. On that very day the young man on the sedan chair arrived. The princess saw her half kerchief which she had given him. She was overjoyed on seeing the young man and took him to the king. He produced the half kerchief and the half hairpin which matched with the other half in the possession of the princess. Then the king believed that this was the right man. The false bridegroom was punished, the wedding was celebrated, and they lived happily ever after.

22

The pole with magic powers

In Yunnan, under the shadow of a mountain range, was a beautiful lake of very clear water. This area was inhabited by the Yi people. All the shepherds of the nearby village used to graze their cattle by the side of the lake where they themselves rested and played. Their cows drank water from the lake whenever they were thirsty.

By chance there were always ninety-nine cows who were brought every morning, to graze there, but by midday, the flock always numbered one hundred and with the hundredth cow a beautiful maiden would appear. At sunset, when the cowherds went home, there would be ninety-nine cows again, and the maiden would disappear. Nobody knew where she came from and where she went. But the cowherds liked her very much, for she knew many things and would tell them many strange stories.

One day, as the maiden was sitting among the cowherds, she told them that if that cow went into the lake, the water would part and make a road. It could also walk on the surface of the water and, riding on its back, one could even cross the great ocean. One single hair from its body could carry the weight of thousands of cows.

After hearing all these amazing stories, the cowherds wanted to know which one was the magic cow. But the maiden would not tell them because she said that only a very honest man could benefit by the information.

One day, when the cowherds were roaming in search of some fruit their cows broke loose and went into somebody's cornfield. The old man in charge of the corn field took up his carrying pole and chased them out one by one. His pole was old and cracked from many years' use and he did not notice that some cow's hair had got caught in the cracks.

At dusk, when he made ready to go home, he hung two bundles of firewood on to his pole as usual.

When he lifted the pole, he was amazed to find it as light as a feather. He added another bundle at each end. It remained light. He heaped on two huge piles, yet it was weightless. He made his way home cheerfully at a merry speed.

From then on the old man cut wood and took it to the city to sell every day. This way he got more money than he needed for food, and more than he had ever had before and for the first time saved some.

One day, when he was on his way to the city to sell his wood, a rich man saw him. This man became very curious when he saw such a big load of firewood being carried and his curiosity became intense when he saw that the lifter of this heavy load was an old man. He wondered how such an old man could carry such a huge load of wood. He went to the cowherd and asked him.

The old man told the rich man that it was a magic pole and that if he did not believe him he could lift it and would know the truth. The rich man lifted the load on the pole and was amazed to find it weightless.

Now this man wanted to buy it from the cowherd and offered five hundred pieces of silver for the pole. At first, the old man did not agree but then, when he thought that so much money would suffice for his lifetime, agreed to part with it.

The rich man was very happy to have the precious pole, and looked at it fondly. But he was sorry to see its condition. It was all cracked and rough. Therefore, he took it to the best carpenter to plane it smooth. After it was done, the man was satisfied with its appearance. It did not occur to him that all the magic cowhairs were planed away.

When he reached home his wife was very surprised to find him so happy. She had to ask him why he was so pleased. He told her that he had bought a magic pole, and would like her to try it. So he put some weights on both sides of the pole. As she tried to lift the pole she found it was too heavy and cried aloud, 'Husband, don't try to make fun of me. This is no magic pole because I could not lift it.' The rich man did not believe his wife. He thought it was the typical female habit of finding fault with anything their husbands do.

Then in order to show his wife the magic powers of the pole, he added more weight to the pole and tried to lift it. But to no avail. The magic had gone out of the pole for ever.

23

The teaching of a lesson

Long, long ago, there lived a farmer in a small village.
He had three sons. The family was very poor. From
morning till evening they worked very hard, but even then
could not make ends meet. One day the farmer called his
three sons and said, 'Dear sons, we cannot go on like this.
We work so hard, but without any positive outcome. For
many days we have not eaten properly. So I have decided
to send one of you to the next village. There is a landlord,
who wants a labourer'. They decided that the eldest son
should go first. But after a few days, he came back
dejected, because the landlord had discharged him, not
finding him able enough. He did not pay him anything.

Then, it was the second son who decided to go. But
after a short while he returned too, without getting a single
cent from the landlord, for, you know, the landlord was
as vicious as a snake and was always up to malicious
tricks.

Somehow the third son discovered what had transpired
and became very angry. He asked his father for permission
to go and work for the landlord.

But the farmer was hesitant to let his youngest son go
and work, because the boy was only a small lad.
Eventually, however, he gave permission reluctantly.

The third son went straight to the landlord's house and
asked for work. The landlord looked the boy from head
to foot, and said, 'So now you have come to try your
luck where your elder brothers have failed. Don't think

it is that easy'. The boy told him that he still wanted to try. The landlord again warned, 'You can try, but remember, you have to carry out all my orders. If you fail in any one, you will not get one cent from me. Don't forget this condition.'

The boy told him that he had understood everything. So he began to work for the landlord. From dawn to dusk he worked in the fields. One day the landlord asked him to go to the bamboo grove on the hill to feed his bullock the bamboo leaves which had just come out. He also told the boy not to pluck the leaves with his hands to feed the bullock. The landlord thought that he could cheat the lad of his wages in this way.

Next morning he drove the animal to the bamboo grove and tied it to one of the bamboos. Then he began to whip it, to make it climb up the bamboo and shouted, 'Up you go, stupid animal'. The poor animal, feeling the lashes on its back, began to moan pitifully and to circle round the bamboos.

People who passed that way laughed and joked about him. But the boy pretended that he had not heard them. However, the landlord also heard about it. He rushed to the spot and saw everything. He shouted at the boy, ordering him to stop beating his animal, but the boy again ignored him and went on beating it. Then he looked at the landlord and said, 'Look sir, how stupid it is. It will never get to the top if I do not hit it.' The landlord was defeated. He cried loudly to the boy that he took back his order.

In the secret recesses of his mind the boy thought that he was going to teach a lesson to this evil landlord.

Though the landlord was beaten, he hated the boy from the marrow of his bones. Day and night he racked his brains to find some way of cheating him of his proper wages.

One day, he told the lad to grow vegetables on the roof top of the house. He was very happy in the anticipation of outwitting the boy. 'Very well sir, it will be done,' said the boy, as carefree as he was on the first day.

Next morning, he woke up very early, took a hoe, put on a straw hat, and went up to the roof. He started to dig into it as he did in the fields. As soon as he hit the roof, broken tiles began to rattle down on the ceiling below where the landlord lay snoring like a pig.

However, he was soon awakened by the noise. He jumped out of his bed and came out dragging his heavy body. He was mad with anger when he saw what was happening. He shouted at the boy and abused him. The lad looked down, and saw the landlord threatening him, but pretended that he had not heard anything.

Again the landlord shouted and ordered him to come down. But the boy coldly told him that he was obeying his order, and was trying to plant vegetables on the roof. The landlord shouted at him and said, 'Did I tell you to break the roof down?' Calmly, the boy told him that he was carrying out his order. In order to plant vegetables he had to dig the roof. If he did not do it, how would the vegetables grow?

The landlord was completely stunned to hear the boy. He shouted to him that he had taken back his order.

The young peasant was satisfied that he had beaten the wicked fellow the second time.

Now the landlord was worried and could not think of any way to deal with the young peasant. But he went on trying to think of some new plan to cheat the peasant of his wages.

And so time passed until the autumn harvest drew near. The weather was dry and hot. The crops were failing for lack of water. One day the landlord said to the boy, 'Because of this drought my crops will die. They must be brought into the house. Tomorrow you are to move the fields into my house'. He eyed the boy cunningly, thinking that this time he was surely going to trap him.

The boy seemed as carefree as ever. Next morning very early, he got up and went to the front door, and broke it down. After that, he broke the door frame, and then started to hew down the wall. The landlord's wife was shocked when she saw what was happening. She ordered the boy to stop at once. The young peasant paid no attention towards her and continued to demolish the wall. The wife ran inside to wake her husband who came running, without even wearing his shirt. He burned with fury when he saw the damaged house. But the lad paid no heed even to his master and kept on hewing at the wall, with all his strength. This drove the landlord completely wild, and he started shouting and abusing him like a mad man.

Calmly, the boy asked the master why he was raving and shouting. How could he expect him to move that large patch of land into the house through a tiny door. The landlord was completely stunned and speechless. With tears in his eyes he took back this order.

Three times the wicked landlord was outwitted. And after that he dared not cheat the peasant of his wages. At the end of the year he paid him a full wage. And after that he never tricked anybody again. Such was the lesson taught by the young peasant.

24
The long-white-haired girl

Long, long ago, there was a small village under the shadow of a high mountain. The biggest problem in this village was that there was no water near this high mountain. People had no alternative but to collect rain water for drinking and irrigation. If it did not rain, they had to walk more than two miles to draw water in buckets from a stream. Water was prized as highly as oil.

In that village, lived a girl with long raven-black hair which reached her heels. Everyone called her the Long-Haired-Girl. She lived with her ailing mother and raised pigs to support them both. Every day she fetched water from the stream over two miles away and then went up the mountain to gather wild herbs for her pigs. She worked very hard from morning till night.

One day she went up the mountain as usual to gather wild herbs. When she was half way, she saw a ripe turnip with lush green leaves, growing on the rock face. She was overjoyed to find a ripe turnip, thinking that it would make a delicious dish for the evening.

She tugged with both hands and pulled the turnip which was red and round and as big as a tea cup. It left a hole in the rock from which a stream of clear spring water began to flow. Suddenly, the turnip jumped out of her hands and landed back in the hole again, blocking the flow of the water.

The Long-Haired-Girl was very thirsty and wanted a drink. She pulled out the turnip again to let the water flow from the hole, and drank her fill. The water was cool and as sweet as fruit juice. But as soon as her mouth left the hole the turnip jumped out of her hands again and landed in the hole blocking the flow of water.

She was standing there on the cliff in amazement, when all of a sudden a gust of wind blew her away to a cave. There, on a huge stone sat a man whose entire body was covered with brown hair. He spoke in his thunderous voice and warned her not to disclose the secret of the sweet water spring. He also warned her that if she told anyone anything about this spring he would kill her. He told her that he was the god of the mountain.

She became very sad, and silently went towards her home. She did not tell anything even to her mother. Without uttering a word she watched the parched fields and the plight of the villagers. Men and women, young and old alike panted and sweated as they carried buckets of water from the stream more than two miles away. She could do nothing. The angry god of the mountain forced her into silence.

She was in great agony of mind. She totally lost her appetite and could not sleep at night. She became like a mute, always staring with her lustreless eyes. Her cheeks lost their glow and became sallow and her shining black hair became dry and brittle. Her mother was greatly concerned at the plight of her daughter, who had been the personification of beauty and health only a few days ago. But now she ignored herself. Her mother asked her the reason for this silent suffering but the Long-Haired-Girl bit her lips and did not say a word.

Her mental agony was so great that within a short spell of time, her raven black hair turned snow white. She neglected her hair, and let it hang loose on her shoulders.

The villagers wondered how a young girl's hair could turn as white as snow. But she had no thought to spare for herself. She was always found staring blankly at the passersby, murmuring to herself: 'On the high mountain there is a . . .' She would never complete the sentence.

One day while she was standing at the gates of her house, she saw an old man tottering along the road carrying a bucket of water which he had brought from the river two miles away. The poor fellow slipped, broke his bucket, spilled the water and badly wounded himself on the knee which was bleeding profusely.

The Long-Haired-Girl ran to help the old man. She dressed his wound with a piece of cloth which she tore off from her skirt. The wrinkled old man was wincing with pain.

The Long-Haired-Girl scolded herself for being such a coward. She thought that she was being very selfish seeing the village folk suffer. It was the fear of death which had prevented her from telling the villagers about the spring on the mountain. But now after seeing the old man, she suddenly changed her mind. She was not frightened of dying anymore.

Suddenly she said to the old man, 'Grandpa, this is the end of the suffering for you and the whole of the village. There is a spring of sweet water on the mountain. What I am saying is the truth. I have seen it with my own eyes and tasted it with my lips'. All the village folk gathered there and she told everybody to follow her over to the mountain with their knives and chisels.

On reaching the spot, where the turnip was growing, she pulled out the turnip and asked the people to cut it into small pieces so that it could not block the hole. The people did what she said. The hole was the size of a cup, from which cool, sweet water began to flow. Then she asked them to widen the hole. At first, when they chiselled the hole, it became the size of a bowl, when they chiselled it again it was the size of a bucket. And finally it was the size of a vat. The water ran gurgling down the mountain, and the villagers laughed, danced and cheered.

Just at that moment a fierce wind blew and the Long-Haired-Girl vanished from sight. The villagers were too busy to notice anything. After sometime, one of them said, 'But where is the Long-Haired-Girl?' Somebody said perhaps she had gone to give the news to her ailing mother.

But we know that the girl had not gone to her mother, but that the poor little thing had been carried away by the god of the mountain to his cave.

The god of the mountain shouted in his thunderous voice and said to the poor scared girl, 'I warned you not to disclose the secret of the sweet water spring. But you disobeyed me and led all those people up here, and now they have chopped up the turnip and widened the hole! I shall kill you for this!'

The White-Haired-Girl told the god of the mountain that she was willing to die, as she could not see her village folk suffering. She also said, 'God of the Mountain, I knew that I would have to die, if I did not keep this secret. But I am prepared to die rather than see people suffering. You can kill me'.

On hearing this, the god of the mountain became more angry and said that he would not let her die easily. He would make her lie on the cliff and let the spring water fall on her body from the high mountain. This painful punishment, he thought, must be given to the Long-Haired-Girl.

The girl did not even wince at this dreadful punishment, but very calmly told him that she was happy that she could make the villagers happy. The punishment was nothing compared to the relief of her village folk. She asked the god to give her a little time so that she could go and see her ailing mother and the pigs.

The god of the mountain told her to go and do whatever she wanted to do. But he reminded her that if she did not come back and do what he had asked her to do, he would kill all the villagers. He also told her that after accomplishing her work she should go and lie down on the cliff and need not bother him again.

The Long-Haired-Girl nodded. A gust of wind blew her down from the cave to the foot of the mountain. There she saw water coming down from the mountain through the fields lush with green crops and she laughed with joy.

When she reached home, she did not have the heart to tell her mother the truth. She said, 'Mother, now we will never need to worry about water again. The villagers are very happy now. Some girls in the next village have invited me to stay and play with them for a few days. I have asked Auntie next door to take care of you and to look after the pigs'.

The mother was very pleased to see her child happy. So she told her to go and enjoy herself.

The Long-Haired-Girl went to the lady next door to arrange her affairs. Before going she again went to her mother. Tears rolled down her cheeks with the thought that she would no longer see her mother. Then she went to pat her pigs. She was sad but felt satisfied.

She climbed the mountain till she saw that half way up stood a big banyan tree with long branches and thick leaves growing by the side of the road. On seeing the tree again her eyes filled with tears because she thought that she would no longer be able to come and cool herself in its shade. Suddenly, she saw an old man coming from behind the tree. He had green hair, a green beard and green clothes.

The old man asked the Long-Haired-Girl where she was going. The girl did not speak but bowed her head in silence. Then the old man said, 'Dear child, I know everything. You are a kind hearted person and I have decided to save you from your troubles. I have carved a girl of stone which resembles you in appearance. Come and have a look yourself and then tell me if I am correct'.

The Long-Haired-Girl went behind the tree and was amazed to see the stone girl, which was absolutely like herself except that it did not have hair. The old man told her that he had carved her image in stone to fool the god of the mountain. He said that he would make the stone girl lie down on the cliff in her place. But he told her that though he had made the image with perfection, there was one major difference. It had no long white hair. So he said to the girl, 'My child you will have to bear pain for a little while. I am going to tear out your white hair and put it on the stone girl's head so that the god of the mountain will not suspect'.

Before the Long-Haired-Girl could protest the old man tore off her hair. Then he put the long white hair on the head of the stone girl. Surprisingly, enough it began to take root as soon as it touched the stone head. The Long-Haired-Girl became hairless. Then the old man told her to go and enjoy herself as the god of the mountain would never trouble her. After saying this, the old man disappeared. Immediately her hair began to grow long and raven black again. Her joy knew no bounds. She danced with happiness.

For a long time, she stood under the tree, waiting for the old man to come back. But the old man did not come. Suddenly, the leaves and branches of the big banyan tree trembled in the breeze making a sound. She heard the words as if they were saying, 'Long-Haired-Girl we have tricked the god of the mountain. You can go home now.' And you know who saved the Long-Haired-Girl from the god of the mountain? None other than the good old banyan tree.

On her return, she saw the long stream of water flowing down the steep mountain, the green crops at the foot of the mountain, the joyous people in the fields and the giant green banyan tree. Swinging her long, shiny raven black hair, she ran back home. The people of the village call this waterfall White Hair Fall.